"I'm... I'm sorry,"
Sarah said quietly.

"I'm not," Dan replied with a shake of his head and an expression that reminded Sarah of the one he'd worn when he'd first seen the rose garden. He was as shocked and as moved by what had happened as she. "I'm not at all sorry," he continued. "I only wish you hadn't stopped... I'm not a patient man, Sarah Turner. I'm used to taking what I want..." He stepped a little way back from her, keeping his hands on her shoulders, and his eyes, filled with longing and a hint of that passion Sarah had just tasted, roamed over her.

"I want you," he said.

To Jean Fauré, *Baltimore is home. While growing up in an extended family, she read voraciously, played softball tirelessly, and studied piano (ambivalently) at the Peabody Conservatory of Music. Writing is an obsession; she's not entirely happy unless she's working on something, but she also takes great pleasure in her husband and son. Her secret wish is . . . to own and operate a tractor-trailer rig!*

Dear Reader:

If the New Year always catches you by surprise, as it does me, you'll especially appreciate this month's SECOND CHANCE AT LOVE romances, which are sure to make the adjustment to 1985 fun and easy. Read on to learn a little bit about each one; in fact, from now on in this space I'll be revealing intriguing tidbits about the current month's books and their authors. Hints about next month's books will still appear on the inside back cover, and we've also added a two-page questionnaire, which I hope you'll fill out. The information you provide will keep us in touch with exactly what kinds of books you most enjoy.

First on the January list is *Knight of Passion* (#238) by Linda Barlow. Judging from the responses we've received, Linda has quickly become one of your favorite writers. In this whimsical, poignant romance, Philippa and Jeff—a pair as modern as they come—begin to suspect they were doomed lovers in another life centuries ago. After all those eons, the two combatants are still literally crossing swords. Talk about long arguments! Also, keep a sharp eye out for Bret and Daniel from Linda's *Bewitched* (#224), who make cameo appearances here.

Frances Davies, another favorite writer, will knock your socks off with *Mysterious East* (#239). A frivolous disguise plunges Karen East into the world's zaniest identity crisis with golden Viking Erik Søndersen, and deceptions pile onto deceptions faster than you can say "Sherlock Holmes." Prepare yourself for the most unusual seduction . . . by artichoke! *Mysterious East* is a thoroughly delectable romp.

Bed of Roses (#240) is by new author Jean Fauré, a gifted dreamweaver who writes with heart-wrenching impact. She also knows the ins and outs of roses—she has a greenhouse in her own back yard. I think you'll find *Bed of Roses* refreshingly different and emotionally involving.

Bridge of Dreams (#241) is another enchanting romance from Helen Carter, author of *Touched by Lightning* (#194), which so many of you praised in your letters. Helen's characters really tug at your heartstrings, and her stories have a way of gently captivating you until you can't put them down. In this book, Liz Forsyth and Josh Gates's urgent involvement proves Helen's powers of seduction once again.

Jean Barrett—another new "Jean" for SECOND CHANCE AT LOVE—has written a breathtakingly sensual and compelling story. *Fire Bird* (#242) begins with a dramatic plane crash on a remote, icebound island and continues with three days of all-consuming passion between Carly and "Skyhawk." A touch of mystery and Skyhawk's imminent departure make this romance particularly effective.

Finally, in *Dear Adam* (#243) Jasmine Craig creates two memorable males—Damion Tanner, whom Lynn Frampton *thinks* she loves, and Adam Hunter, whom you'll *know* she loves. Once again, Jasmine creates strong sexual tension with skillful subtlety. And don't feel too bad about Damion—you just may see more of him later!

Be sure to treat yourself well this January by escaping the holiday confusion and relaxing with all six SECOND CHANCE AT LOVE romances. Before you know it, you'll be writing 1985 instead of 1984 on your correspondence, and you'll realize you've adjusted to a new beginning after all!

Warm wishes for a Happy New Year!

Ellen Edwards

Ellen Edwards, Senior Editor
SECOND CHANCE AT LOVE
The Berkley Publishing Group
200 Madison Avenue
New York, N.Y. 10016

Second Chance at Love ®

BED OF ROSES

JEAN FAURÉ

SECOND CHANCE AT LOVE
BOOK

Second Chance at Love books are published by
The Berkley Publishing Group
200 Madison Avenue, New York, NY 10016

- *1* -

"SARAH, TOM WANTS you out in section three." Betty Connors's head appeared around the edge of the open office door. The older woman with the salt-and-pepper hair went on to explain with a woeful look, "Looks like trouble with the water again."

Sarah Turner dropped her pencil onto the ledger sheet in front of her. "All right," she said, sighing. "I'm on my way, but don't expect me to have these accounts done for you this afternoon."

Betty chuckled as she disappeared. "You don't think I really expected to see them, do you?"

"Such confidence," Sarah grumbled as she grabbed her sun hat off the coat rack and followed Betty into the main office. She was glad there weren't any clients there to witness her disgust over the faulty irrigation system. It would have been difficult to paste on the obligatory smile.

"Don't worry about the accounts," Betty said kindly

1

as Sarah passed her desk on the way out the front door. "I'll finish them up myself."

Sarah looked back over her shoulder and replied gratefully, "Thanks, Betts. I'll try to do better tomorrow." And then the door closed behind her and she was no longer in an air-conditioned office but outside on a hot, Maryland spring day.

Sarah pulled her keys from the pocket of her slacks as she walked toward the line of pickups behind the office. The colors of Sarah's blouse and slacks—mint and dark green—were echoed in the dozen or so vehicles, with the darker color emblazoned boldly on the cab doors in letters that read ASHCROFT NURSERY. Sarah's pickup was the smallest in the row, and she soon had it bouncing over the dirt road that led into the southwest corner of her property.

Despite the heat and the nuisance of having her irrigation system on the blink again, Sarah was glad for the excuse to leave the office. Running the nursery alone was more work than she'd ever dreamed possible, but the worst was keeping track of the books. Taking care of the stock itself was hard, but it was never tedious or boring. Her father had felt the same way—and that was why he'd had a partner. Henry Turner and Kent Ashcroft had made a good team.

Sarah's heart was tugged by a familiar twinge of remorse as she thought of her late husband, Bill Turner, Henry's son; she and Bill hadn't made a very good team, either as business or marriage partners. They'd tried for six years, and maybe eventually they would have worked things out as far as the business was concerned; but the marriage, she was certain, would always have been a loss. In any event, there would be no chance to find out. Bill had died of heart failure the previous spring at the age of forty, only four years after she had lost her father. It was now up to Sarah to carry on the family business.

The rows of butternut trees that led back into section three of the nursery ended, and Sarah pulled the pickup to a stop alongside Tom Swenson's larger truck. Before getting out, she put her broad-brimmed straw hat on top of her honey-blond head and tied the scarf that held it on, knotting it under her chin. The hat hid a great deal—the shoulder-length knot of silky hair, the emerald-green almond-shaped eyes, the high cheekbones and porcelain skin. In fact, all that could be seen of Sarah's features under the brim were her classic bow lips and her chin. Thus protected, she hopped out of the truck and looked down the long rows of budding rose bushes—some just starting to show color, others already covered with their first blooms of the season. She located Tom and made her way between two rows of crimson blooms, calling his name.

"Tom! Betty said you needed me."

A wiry, weather-beaten man of about fifty-five squatted in the center of the rose field, working over a complex set of pipe fittings. He looked up when Sarah called, then pushed back his hat and waved to her. They met halfway down the row of bushes.

"It's the damned pipes," Tom said with a frustrated shake of his balding head. "At least I think it is. I can't get water out here at all, and if I can't fix it soon, I think you'd better call Jenkins. There might be a break I can't find, and these bushes can't go another day without water."

Sarah scanned the roses with a practiced eye. Tom was right. The newer growth showed signs of wilting. "Let's try once more, and then I'll go back and call before it gets too late," she suggested. She gave her nursery manager an encouraging smile from under the brim of her hat.

"Okay, you're the boss," Tom nodded. "Go get that box of wrenches from the back of my truck and bring 'em back to the main coupling."

"Are you *sure* I'm the boss?" Sarah grinned impishly over her shoulder as she ran back to do his bidding. Tom Swenson had been working at the nursery since before Sarah was born. Now that she was the owner, they got along very well, with Tom recognizing her expertise in horticulture and Sarah recognizing his instinctive knowledge of green and growing things. Together they kept the rest of the regular crew of gardeners on track. She had a similar relationship with Betty Connors, who had also been at Ashcroft for thirty years. Betty ran the office and Sarah tried to stay out of her way. Life went on in this fashion much as it had since Kent Ashcroft started Ashcroft Nursery. Sarah knew it wouldn't matter who owned the place—Betty and Tom would run it as they had been doing all along.

Tom and Sarah worked over the recalcitrant irrigation pipes for over an hour. When Sarah glanced at her watch and saw it was four-thirty, she sat back on her heels and looked at Tom questioningly. "Shall we give up?"

"What will you do if I say yes?" he asked.

"Call Jenkins to come fix it and then tell Cecelia she'll have to cancel the order for orchids she handed me this morning." Sarah's answer was unhesitant but her disappointment was clear.

Tom smiled. Like Sarah, he knew that calling Jenkins meant spending money on repairs that could be better spent in other ways.

"Let's give it one more try, boss," he said. "You keep working on this coupling. I'm going to go try something else. I've got a hunch..."

"Okay." Sarah nodded halfheartedly. It was true she didn't want to spend more money on repairs, but as she pulled at the clinging fabric of her mint-green blouse and squinted up at the hot afternoon sun, calling Jenkins began to seem like a very sensible idea. She ran the back of one delicate, small-boned hand across her dripping forehead, wiped her palms on her slacks, and picked up the wrench and regulator valve once more.

For several minutes Sarah tried to get the regulator onto the coupling. And then, quite suddenly, a volcano erupted before her eyes. Instinctively she protected her face with her hands as she fell backward, landing squarely on her bottom. Stunned, Sarah uncovered her face— now dripping wet like the rest of her, and getting wetter—and looked skyward.

"Hallelujah," she muttered in somewhat dubious relief. Then she extricated herself from the rose bush she'd fallen against and which had hooked onto her blouse, and she recovered her hat, which had been blown off. Never mind that she was drenched to the skin; she had to find the regulator—the one that had been blasted away—and she had to fasten it on! The water, which was now gushing from the pipe like a Texas oil well, had to be directed into the ground and off the leaves of the bushes.

"You all right?"

It was Tom's voice calling as he ran toward her from the main drive. Sarah jumped to her feet. "I'm fine!" she called. "Bring another regulator out here. The old one went with Mount St. Helens!"

Ten minutes later the two of them trudged out of section three toward the pickups, both of them soaked to the skin and laughing. Tom stuck out his hand for Sarah to shake. "That was mighty fine work, boss," he said. "I'll be sure to call you next time I need a plumber."

"I'll be sure not to be home!" she retorted with a grin. And then she stopped short as her gaze took in a gleaming white Mercedes and the sinfully attractive man leaning against it. Her grin faded. "Oh, Lord," she groaned.

"Never saw him before," Tom answered her unspoken question.

"I'll bet he's from the bank," Sarah hazarded a guess. "But how did he get here?"

"Must be important," Tom said.

"That's what I'm afraid of," she mumbled, and looked down at her wet garments.

"Uh, I'll see you later." Cheerfully Tom saluted, then moved off toward the larger pickup.

"Deserter," Sarah hissed accusingly as she walked slowly toward the man who had parked by her truck.

"The woman in the office told me I might find Sarah Turner out here." The man's smooth baritone left a distinct question lingering in the air, as did his look of amused disbelief when she stopped before him.

Sarah stared at him for a moment, hoping she conveyed the appropriate note of displeasure over the fact that he was wandering around, unescorted, in her nursery. Blue eyes—very blue, like the sky—stared back at her. And there was a lock of thick, rich brown hair falling forward over the dark brows, accentuating his outrageously long lashes. The slightly upturned nose and wide, sensual mouth were somehow incongruent with the rest of his sophisticated appearance. Her eyes traveled downward briefly to take in the dark blue slacks and light blue European-cut shirt that covered his lean-hipped, broad-shouldered frame. He'd taken off his dark jacket and now held it slung over one shoulder as he waited for her reply. He wasn't an especially tall man—somewhere around five feet ten, she guessed—but Sarah shivered a little in the face of such a mixture of undeniable male attractiveness and boyishly melting charm. Her gaze returned to meet his as she answered finally, "Betty was right. You've found me."

The smile left his face immediately. *"You're* Sarah Turner?"

"That's right." Sarah nodded curtly. She was certain this man was from the bank. She was late with a payment and they'd already called twice that week.

"I don't believe it," the man stated flatly and with a hint of the arrogance his appearance indicated he was capable of displaying.

Sarah was not normally rude. It was her business to cultivate good public relations, after all. But this was too much.

"Look here, sir," she began in a tightly controlled voice, wishing he wouldn't look at her so intently. "I just finished a rather unpleasant afternoon's work. I'm hot and hungry and soaking wet. I don't know who you are, but *nobody* is supposed to be out here. I don't know how you talked Betty into telling you where I was, but if you've got business with me, I'd suggest you go back to the office and wait. And if you expect to see somebody else behind Sarah Turner's desk, you might as well leave now. I'm all you'll get."

Sarah stalked over to the pickup, yanked open the door, and grabbed a towel off the front seat. She was furiously scrubbing her face and arms when she heard a low chuckle behind her. The sound stopped her for a moment and her eyes narrowed. Tossing the towel back onto the seat, she turned slowly.

"Do you need directions?" she asked caustically.

"No," he replied, his voice quite pleasant, in contrast. "Tell me,"—his head tilted slightly—"besides owning Ashcroft and serving as its chief plumber, do you also do your own public-relations work?"

That did it.

"Who are you?" Sarah demanded. "If you're from the bank, I've already talked to them twice this week, and I have nothing more to say."

"You aren't going to like this," the man said with a sad shake of his head.

"You are from the bank?"

"Uh-uh," he said almost apologetically.

"Well, what, then?"

"Are you sure you want to know? Wouldn't you rather wait until you're, uh, feeling a little less indisposed?" His intense blue gaze gave her back some of what she'd given him as it raked her from head to toe thoroughly, shockingly, not missing a single drop of water and lingering on the curves her clinging wet clothing revealed.

Sarah bristled under the scrutiny and realized, to her horror, that her body was reacting traitorously to the man's inspection. She felt the nipples of her high, firm breasts harden against the fabric of her bra and knew he must see it, too. She also knew that her nearly white skin was turning quite disgustingly red. What embarrassed her further was that, when he finally returned his gaze to hers, he looked disappointingly unaffected—until he grinned. And then Sarah's world fell apart. Two rows of absolutely perfect white teeth were revealed in a face that was lit with rakish delight. It was a knowing grin. It was disarming. It was probably the sexiest smile Sarah had ever seen, and she felt herself grow even warmer.

"Who are you?" she insisted, angry at the nervous

flutter his look caused in her stomach.

"You asked for it." He shrugged. "Remember, I gave you the chance to retreat."

"I said, who are . . . ?"

"Daniel Lowell."

Behind them, the water in the irrigation system gushed through the silence. The only other sound was made by a big horse fly that buzzed around their heads. Sarah swiped at the fly absently.

Suddenly the name connected.

"You're Daniel Lowell?" she breathed incredulously.

"You've got it." He smiled crookedly. "Your new neighbor."

Sarah stared a moment longer. And then she said, "I don't believe it."

He laughed out loud. "Look, how about you and I go get out of this sun and find you some dry clothes? When the real Sarah Turner and Dan Lowell turn up, we'll let them finish this argument. Okay?"

With the memory of her rude speech and the shock of him standing before her, actually laughing, Sarah contemplated how delightful it would be just to faint—wondered if she could use the heat as an excuse . . . But it wasn't *that* hot. She groaned inwardly and searched for the words to apologize. It would have been bad enough if he really had been from the bank, or even a stranger off the street. But no, he was Daniel Lowell, multimillionaire, land baron, and the head of Lowell Industrial Corporation. LINC, as it was called, had just bought an enormous tract of land—woods and farms, for the most part—to the south and east of her own property. The plan was to turn the tract into a new town, a model city; all the newspapers were filled with the talk. Local firms were putting in bids for the construction. Professional services were vying for space in buildings not even begun. Indeed, the Maryland suburbs north of Washington, D.C., were rolling out the red carpet in anxious anticipation of the arrival of LINC. And of all the impossible things, she had just told the man who was LINC itself to go to hell.

"Oh, dear," Sarah muttered with a pained look.

Dan caught the exclamation and the look of despair. "Come, now," he said brightly. "It can't be that bad. Frankly, I wish to hell I was drenched right now, too. It's got to be better than this heat. And I probably deserved everything you said for being such an overbearing jerk. I should've waited for you at the office."

Sarah shook her head. "No, I'm awfully sorry, Mr. Lowell. I don't know what came over me. I guess I was just taking my frustration over the irrigation problems out on you."

"Can we have this apology someplace else?" he asked. "As embarrassing as it is to have to admit it, I sunburn easily." With a peek under the brim of her hat, he added, "I don't imagine you fare much better."

"Of course!" Sarah nodded. "Would you like to follow me back to the office? It's rather late, but..." She hesitated. "Why *are* you here, Mr. Lowell?"

"I'm afraid what I want will have to wait." He grinned, and there was just enough innuendo in his voice to make Sarah feel uncomfortable, but still leave her uncertain of what he meant. "Your secretary said you'd probably be going straight home from here," he continued, "so I suppose I should stop back tomorrow morning."

It was a combination of guilt over her behavior, appreciation for the gracious way he had taken the whole thing and the effort he was making to make her feel comfortable, and outright curiosity that made Sarah say impulsively, "Oh, I couldn't let you do that. Why don't you follow me home. I live just over on the other side of the property. I'll change my clothes and then you can tell me what business LINC has with Ashcroft Nursery."

He hesitated only momentarily. "If you're sure..." Then, when she nodded, he said, "Lead the way." And he grinned once more before striding jauntily back to his car.

All the way down the dirt road that wound through the nursery to her house, on the nursery's southern boundary, Sarah stole glances through the rearview mirror at the white car following her. What on earth could he want? Surely, he didn't make a point of meeting all his "neighbors" personally. She still shivered, in spite of the heat, when she thought about those blue eyes boring into her—into her very soul, it seemed. In all her life, she'd never felt as completely naked as she did under his gaze. She could have walked around naked in front of her husband, and nine times out of ten he wouldn't have noticed. But this man . . . Yes, he made her want to put on a winter coat, to hell with the eighty-nine-degree mercury reading.

And yet . . . and yet, all the while he was making her nervous, he was going out of his way to put her at ease. He was charming—overwhelmingly so.

The two vehicles pulled to a halt simultaneously beneath the spreading white oak in Sarah's front yard. The tree was well over a hundred years old, and enormous. And although there were many ornamental shrubs and roses planted around the house, the oak was the only tree in the yard. The nursery trees, however, were never far away; and all one had to do was cast a roving eye over the horizon, and Ashcroft greenery of one sort or another stretched for as far as one could see.

"What a beautiful old house!" Dan exclaimed, getting out of his car and coming up beside Sarah.

Sarah looked at the white Victorian structure with a loving eye. "I've lived in it all my life," she said. "My father was raised here, and so was his mother. It needs a little paint right now, but I love it." Without waiting for his next comment, Sarah continued, "Come inside. Would you like some iced tea or lemonade while you wait?"

"That would be wonderful," he replied as they walked toward the front steps. "I'll be glad to get it myself, though, while you change. Just point me toward the kitchen."

Sarah glanced at him as they reached the front door. He certainly did not behave as she thought a millionaire land developer should. *Just point me toward the kitchen.* Who was he kidding? She shrugged to herself. Well, even millionaire land developers got thirsty, didn't they?

"It's through that door." She gestured toward the back of the house, down the long entrance hall. The polished oak floors were mostly bare, with an occasional Oriental rug providing color and warmth. "The drinks are in the refrigerator. I'll be just a few minutes. Please make yourself comfortable." And she was sure he would.

Dan gave her a friendly salute and disappeared into the kitchen. Sarah stared after him, feeling puzzled and vaguely excited. The man did strange things to her senses, and as she watched the door swinging shut on its hinges she felt the first stabs of danger.

Twenty minutes after walking into the house, Sarah had showered, blow dried her hair, and put on a touch of mascara and lip gloss; now she was rooting through the armoire in her Victorian-style bedroom. She discarded the notion of dressing in another set of work clothes and chose instead a bright yellow sun dress with a full skirt and a halter top. Not exactly a dress for a business conference—and what else could Dan Lowell want to talk but business?—but a little voice in the back of her mind urged her to contradict his first impression of her as best she could. She didn't twist her hair into its convenient knot but pulled the two sidepieces back with tortoiseshell combs, leaving the long, golden strands to fluff over her bare shoulders. Slipping her feet into a pair of white sandals, she hurried down the stairs and into the living room, where she expected Dan to be.

He wasn't there. The grandfather clock ticked quietly in the empty room. The Sheraton sofa and wing chairs grouped around the fireplace were empty. With a slight frown, Sarah crossed the room and peeked through the doorway to the den to find Dan examining her father's award plaques on the wall above the fireplace.

Dan heard—or sensed—her watching, and turned. "This is all very impress—" His eyes widened at the sight of her, and with quiet emphasis, he exclaimed, "My God!"

Sarah, who had been walking toward him, stopped

short. His reaction to her was so startling that it made her look down to see that everything was, indeed, where it belonged. She looked back at him to find him still staring at her as though she were an apparition. "Is something wrong?" she asked.

Dan recovered himself with difficulty and shook his head. "Not a thing. Are you *sure* you're Sarah Turner?"

The look on his face was designed to melt the most disgruntled of souls, and Sarah couldn't resist a tiny smile. With one hand on a slender hip, she said, "I'm sorry, but she got lost in the shower. You'll have to settle for me instead."

"If this is settling..." Dan came across the room quickly to stop a foot in front of her. With one hand holding a glass of iced tea, he reached out to tilt her chin upward. "I never would have believed it," he said softly as he met her gaze. "Who would have guessed what was under than silly hat?" When a look of mild exasperation crossed Sarah's features, he smiled and added, "I'm sorry for staring. It's every Irishman's dream to meet a leprechaun, and I'd already counted myself fortunate. But I had no idea leprechauns could turn themselves into angels." His blue eyes caressed her·as though he were convinced she was capable of such magic.

Sarah's heart ground to a halt. Her breath caught in her throat and she tore her head out of his light grasp in order to step away. Casting her eyes around the room, she saw an unattended glass of iced tea that he'd apparently poured for her. She grabbed it quickly with a stiff, "Thank you for the tea."

"Now what have I done wrong?" Dan asked.

"Nothing... It's just that... that I'm not used to... I don't normally..." Sarah whirled to face him again. "Why *are* you here, Mr. Lowell?"

"Dan, please," he corrected. "We're neighbors, after all—and that's reason enough to come over and introduce myself." He shrugged. "However, there happens to be another reason. You see, I've known about the Ashcroft Nursery for years. You've got quite a reputation."

He looked to her for acknowledgment of his statement.

Sarah nodded. "Yes, but I had no idea that our name had made its way into the upper echelons of the New York business community."

"You'd be amazed at what some of us do in our spare time." He winked conspiratorially. "Plants have a very soothing effect on nerves made raw by watching the stock exchange all day long."

"I can imagine," Sarah remarked, and then, realizing that she hadn't even offered him a seat, she said quickly, "Would you like to sit in here? Or would you prefer the porch, where it's cooler?"

"Actually"—he turned to look at the wall plaques once more—"I'd like to look at these. Tell me about Ashcroft. I know your father founded the nursery some forty years ago, but I gathered from your secretary that he's no longer living."

"He died five years ago," Sarah replied, walking around to the other side of the big cherry desk to stand beside him and look at the plaques. She hesitated, not quite sure of what to say. Dan Lowell made her incredibly uncomfortable. And it seemed safe to attribute her state to the fact that she had little experience dealing with men like him. Foreign diplomats and elected officials and all shapes, sizes, and varieties of lawyers and other professionals, yes. Such persons constituted the bulk of the population of the District of Columbia. But Wall Street tycoons? Decidedly not. And strangely enough, she felt a little as she had on her first date—excited, nervous, and torn between wishing he'd follow through on the look in his eyes and wishing she could just disappear.

"What would you like to know about Ashcroft?" she asked, calmly enough. "You don't really want me to give you a detailed description of how my father traveled all over the world to collect specimen trees and shrubs for propagation, do you?"

Dan laughed. "The travels of a horticulturist? It would make fascinating listening, but I'm afraid the finer points would be lost on me. What I really want is to see your roses." And he turned to look at her, his sky-blue eyes suddenly intense, fueled by some inner excitement. "I have this . . . this passion about roses, you see." He searched her face as though expecting to hear that of course she did see. "I want dozens and dozens of them planted outside my office and my home in the new town when it's completed."

"You're going to be living down here?" Sarah asked, surprised at the news. The newspaper accounts hadn't mentioned this.

Dan nodded. "This town is only the first of many I hope to build. It's different from what LINC has done in the past, but it's been my dream for many years, and I intend to make this first town my home. I have to admit"—he smiled—"that when I bought the tract, I was well aware that your nursery was here. It was a deciding factor in my choice of properties."

Sarah was stunned. "You're not serious."

"Oh, I'm very serious. I kept thinking about those roses you're so famous for." His gaze dropped briefly to her lips, which were parted slightly in astonishment. "Now I'm more sure than ever I've made the right decision."

Sarah blinked and felt herself blushing. She held his gaze for another instant and then had to look away.

"Mr. Lowell . . . Dan, I don't know what to say. I'm very flattered . . . That is, Ashcroft is very flattered and a little overwhelmed at such praise. It's late for a tour today, but perhaps tomorrow?" She looked back at him, one finely arched brow raised in question.

Dan chuckled, obviously aware of her attempt to avoid the personal implication his words had conveyed. "Tomorrow will be fine," he said. "I came to D.C. two weeks before the rest of the office moved so I could become acclimated to my new environment. For once, there's nothing I absolutely must do. My time is my own—until my secretary arrives with my appointment book, Then I go back into slavery."

Sarah gave him a look of dubious sympathy. How

could one feel sorry for a man who had everything? "Tomorrow, then," she agreed. Then, hesistantly, she added, "Look here, I could at least show you some of the awards and publications and tell you something about the roses. Then you'll know what to look for tomorrow ... That is, if you're interested."

"I'd love to hear about them," he replied enthusiastically.

And so, for the next hour, Dan sat at Sarah's father's desk while she told him about the Ashcroft roses. Using photos and brochures from carefully kept albums, she described all of the patented varieties for which Ashcroft had achieved renown. The albums also contained pictures of her father and herself, news articles about Ashcroft, and letters from people all over the country describing their experiences with particular roses. It was clear that Dan was enthralled, and Sarah soon found herself giving him a condensed version of the history of Ashcroft itself—how her father had gone about establishing the nursery with funds inherited from his grandmother, on land that had been in his family since the Civil War. From the beginning, Ashcroft had specialized in roses as well as unusual trees and shrubs. It was easy talking about these things; it was harder to answer Dan's questions about herself—her work in hybridization; her degree in horticulture; how she juggled her time between roses, the nursery stock, and the greenhouses.

On the whole, however, talking about her work had made it easy to forget just exactly who Dan was and that he was sitting in her home—in her father's chair—looking as though he belonged there. It was all so very comfortable; and yet, there was nothing comfortable about it. After an hour of living with her conflicting feelings, Sarah's hands began to shake as she handed Dan newspaper clippings and turned pages in albums for him to read.

It was more than she could stand when she dropped one of the albums while replacing it on its shelf. Dan immediately stooped by her side to help pick up the scattered pictures. His leg brushed hers, and the smell of his spicy cologne made her head feel light. When she handed him a stack of pictures and his fingers brushed hers briefly, she snatched her hand away and stood quickly.

"Leave the rest of it," she said briskly. "I'll get them later. That was the last album, anyway."

Dan rose to his feet, studying closely the play of emotions on Sarah's pale face. Abruptly, as though he knew of the reasons for her discomfort, he said, "Yes, well, I really should be going. I've kept you long enough."

Sarah muttered something polite and ushered him to the front porch. When he turned to offer his hand, she took it hesitantly.

"Thank you for the picture tour," he said, letting his eyes dip briefly to her mouth before adding, "I'm looking forward to the real thing tomorrow."

Sarah found herself staring at him again, and her hand felt weak in his warm, firm grasp. She knew she was behaving stupidly, but she was utterly confused by her own feelings and by Dan's mixed signals. What did he want from her? All they'd talked about was the business, but his eyes were speaking something quite different. Under other circumstances, had he been anyone else, she would never have tolerated being eyed so openly—would have issued a heated dismissal long before this. And there had been men before and since Bill's death—clients, mostly—who'd tried to break through her reserve. Sarah realized that, if she hadn't been trying to make up to Dan for being so rude, she would never have subjected herself to such a prolonged visit under such duress...

Dan hesitated, as though he were about to say something else. Then he dropped her hand quickly and started down the steps. "About what time would you like me to meet you tomorrow?" he asked.

"Is nine-thirty A.M. all right?" she suggested to his broad, retreating back.

"I'll meet you at your office," he replied. Then, half-way to his car, he turned to wave, giving her another of those earth-shattering smiles. "See you then!"

Sarah nodded. She remained on the porch, watching as the Mercedes sped down the long drive that led to the house from the main road. Her stomach was one mass of knots. Her rational mind knew that nothing had transpired that should have put her in such a state. Their conversation had been perfectly harmless. If anything, she should be flattered by his interest and elated at the prospects of selling rose bushes to Daniel Lowell, president and chairman of the board of Lowell Industrial Corporation. Why, then, did she find herself wishing he was coming to see *her* tomorrow, and not her roses?

- 2 -

SARAH BREEZED INTO the office the next morning at nine o'clock—an hour late—her low-heeled white sandals clicking lightly across the terra-cotta tiled floor. She was wearing a very simple and utterly feminine white sleeveless voile dress with an open neck and a dark green belt that emphasized her narrow waist and slender hips. Her hair was loose around her shoulders, where it clung like shinging spun gold.

Betty took one look at her and gaped. "What's the occasion?" she asked.

Sarah beamed at her office manager as she poured herself a cup of coffee from the pot behind Betty's desk. "We have a visitor coming for a guided tour of the nursery."

"Since when do you get all dressed up for clients?" Betty asked with her eyes narrowed in suspicion behind her reading glasses.

"It's too hot for dark slacks," Sarah pointed out defensively.

18

"It wasn't too hot yesterday," Betty retorted.

Then the door opened and Tom Swenson walked in. "Good Lord!" he exclaimed, giving Sarah the once-over with a somewhat fatherly and not altogether approving eye.

"That's what I say," Betty joined in. "She's got company coming."

"Who?" Tom asked curiously.

"Will you two stop it," Sarah said disgustedly. "I'm sick of wearing nursery uniforms everyday. And Mr. Lowell is just coming to look at roses..."

"Mr. Lowell?" Betty cried in real distress. "Not that arrogant Irishman who was here yesterday!"

"That 'arrogant Irishman' is the head of LINC," Sarah countered. "I was quite rude to him when he caught me . . . er, indisposed out in section three."

Tom laughed. "So he's the one. Well, now I know why you're all dressed up."

"My appearance is none of your business," Sarah said tartly. "The man owns half the county and is going to be investing quite a lot of money in the business community here—handing out building contracts and the like. It behooves us to treat him nicely." She gave the others a meaningful look. "He wants a tour of the rose fields and is interested in buying some for his personal use."

Tom sighed. "Too bad he doesn't want to buy trees."

"Dream on," Sarah laughed shortly, second-guessing Tom's fantasy. "Some commercial landscaper—Tyler or Barron, most likely—will get the landscaping contract, and Mr. Lowell's new town will be planted very properly in standard white pine, sea-green juniper, and eight-foot silver maples. Maybe they'll throw in a few ornamentals here and there on the main streets."

"As much as I love them," Tom said as he poured his own coffee, "sometimes I'd like to plow under all them monsters your daddy planted. They just keep getting bigger and bigger."

"And harder and harder to sell," Sarah added. "Yes,

I know. But we're doing okay, Tom. Business is good."

"Hmph!" Betty interjected. "That's a matter of opinion. I'm with Tom. You get rid of some of that stuff and plant some things that sell quick so you can pay the bills and buy new equipment that doesn't break down."

Sarah sighed. They were both right—they always were—and yet, she tried to ignore the fact that the trees and specialty plants that had been her father's passion were becoming an albatross around her neck. Secretly, she dreamed of having more space for roses; they were her own special interest. She wanted to step up her hybridization research and just didn't have the acreage.

"Well, now that I've had my morning lecture," she said brightly, walking toward her office door, "I think I'll wait for Mr. Lowell in private. Let me know when he arrives."

Sarah tried to work at her desk. She pulled out the ledger sheets for the greenhouses and applied herself to balancing them for all of ten minutes. But her gaze kept wandering out the window, where she expected to see a white Mercedes pull into the parking lot. She fidgeted with her pencil and stared at the columns before her. Finally, with a sigh of resignation, she sank back in the big leather chair and gave up trying to work.

She looked around her office, trying to see it as Dan Lowell would. Tacky, she thought. No, that wasn't fair. The big leather couch, the wooden file cabinets, and the monstrous dark oak desk weren't tacky; they were just old. The only new thing in the room was the sand-colored carpet she'd installed to cover the tile floor. Her father hadn't cared about carpet—hadn't spent enough time behind his desk for it to matter. But she cared, and when it became her office, she'd planned to redecorate the whole thing. She'd just never gotten around to it. Still, it was comfortable, familiar; like all of Ashcroft, it was home.

Soon, Sarah found her attention traveling back out the window, where the morning sunshine was dancing through the sycamore tree that grew on the southeast side of the low brick building. She thought about all those lovely acres of trees that stretched beyond her line of vision, some of them quite rare. There were dawn redwoods and black walnuts and countless varieties of ornamentals. There were also the acres of roses, the care of which she supervised herself. Eight greenhouses sat in a line behind the office building, and there Cecelia Appleby ruled with an iron fist over the care and feeding of all manner of plants. Ferns, violets, and orchids were Cecelia's special loves, and those abounded; but in the spring and fall Ashcroft also sold houseplants and perennials, the chief characteristics of which were that they were hard to find and, often as not, harder to grow. Sarah kept one greenhouse for herself and had had a fair amount of success in cross-pollenating violets. She'd had a white and lavender one with variegated leaves patented the year before. Playing with violets was a hobby, though; the roses were her life's work.

Ashcroft Nursery required every ounce of attention and energy she had to keep it running. It afforded her little time for herself. Tom and Betty reminded her all too often just how much work there was. And in the past, she'd never had cause to resent the work. In fact, in the years after her father died, when it became clear that her marriage would never be more than a business arrangement, her work had filled in huge gaps of loneliness and eased her deep-seated fear that she hadn't been woman enough to inspire Bill to love her.

As a child, she'd idolized Bill Turner; it had never occurred to her that there was anything but love involved when he'd asked her to marry him. And it was a bitter disappointment to discover that he didn't love her. By the time she'd realized the truth about her marriage, it was too late. She'd been a pawn in a business deal planned by well-meaning but decidedly short-sighted parents from the time when she and Bill were youngsters.

Bill had never been unfaithful to her and had treated her with respect. They'd been friends, after all. It was just that Sarah had always expected to fall in love, and she'd made the terrible mistake of assuming that her husband should also be in love with her. When Bill died, Sarah grieved for him as she might for any other friend. Truthfully, her life changed very little with his passing. She still worked ten hours a day; she still had trouble keeping up with the bills the nursery incurred. She still didn't have much of a social life—a few friends from school, a few childhood playmates now with their own families. And she still felt terribly lonely at times. No, not much had changed.

Sarah's gaze dropped down to the envelope that had been lying on her desk for two weeks. It was a letter from Jane Turner, Bill's mother. Jane and Henry had gone to live in Oregon after Bill died. Henry had been unable to bear the nursery after losing both his best friend and his son. Jane was the only mother Sarah had known, her own having died at her birth; and there were times when she missed Jane more than anyone. This letter, like all of Jane's others, was an invitation to come visit. And, as she had all the others, Sarah would answer it by saying she didn't have time to take a trip, but that she would try that winter when business slowed down.

Sarah also thought about the letter that had lain in her top desk drawer for the past six months. It was a job offer from Ryan and Roth in northern California. Ryan and Roth was an internationally known rose nursery, and the president of the company wanted her to come work for them. She'd toyed with the idea only in passing. She could never sell Ashcroft. It was her legacy; it was the only home she'd ever known. Besides, there were other people to consider. Tom Swenson and Betty Connors, for instance. And if those reasons weren't enough, why should she invent new roses for somebody else when she could do it for herself? Because the cost of doing it for herself was rapidly getting to be more than she could afford . . .

Fortunately, Sarah didn't have to dwell on unpleasant realities any longer. Her heart skipped a beat and her attention came immediately back to the present when a small white Mercedes zipped into her line of vision and pulled to a stop at the far side of the lot. She watched as Dan Lowell got out and shut the door, shoved his keys into the pocket of his white slacks, and walked briskly across the lot toward the building. Already she could feel her stomach knotting. This would never do. The man would start to think she was half-witted if she behaved as she had the previous afternoon.

Determined to be her most gracious, informative, and businesslike self, Sarah rose from her desk and went to greet him. Betty was just about to buzz her on the intercom when Sarah walked out of her office.

"Oh..." Betty gave Sarah a dark look and added disappointedly, "There you are."

"I saw Mr. Lowell drive in." Sarah ignored Betty's look and smiled as she extended her hand to Dan in greeting. "I hope you're prepared to walk this morning," she said. "I intend to give you the grand tour."

"If you keep smiling like that, I'll do anything you say." Dan took Sarah's offered hand in both of his and gave her his heart-stopping smile.

Betty sat at her desk and scowled. Tom leaned against the wall next to the coffee pot and raised one bushy gray eyebrow.

"Will you be getting the greenhouse ledger sheets to me sometime today, Sarah?" Betty asked pointedly.

Sarah turned slowly so that Dan couldn't see the look she gave Betty. "Do you need them?" she asked, making it clear the answer had best be no.

Betty's scowl deepened and she turned back to her typewriter, although there was nothing in it at the moment. "If I have to manage without them, I will," she said in the spirit of a true martyr.

"Shall we go?" Dan asked brightly.

Sarah nodded and they began walking toward the door.

Tom stopped them, saying, "You gonna want me to keep the crew out of your way today, boss?"

Sarah turned her back on Dan once again and looked at Tom as though she would like to strangle him. "Why would the crew be in my way, Tom?" she asked with patience that she didn't feel.

"Oh, I don't know. Just thought you might want us to . . . get lost." He reached up to tilt the beak of his green hat back on his head as he insolently looked Dan up and down.

"You just go about your business, Tom," Sarah said quickly, knowing she was turning red with embarrassment. "This is a perfectly normal workday. Is that clear?" Without waiting for an answer, she gave Betty and Tom both a final warning glare and hurried out the door, which Dan was holding for her.

Sarah couldn't bring herself to look at him, so she went quickly toward the row of pickups parked behind the building. Dan caught up to her and matched her strides.

"Have those two known you long?" he asked casually.

"Since I was born," she muttered.

"That explains it, then," he sighed, as though in complete understanding. "They're protecting you from disaster."

"Disaster?" Sarah glanced at him in surprise. "Why on earth . . . ?" But her words trailed off as her eyes met his, which were twinkling with knowing delight. His gaze dropped briefly to scan her attire and came back to linger a moment on her lips. He smiled slowly and then met her gaze once more. "You know very well why they're worried, Sarah," he said quietly.

She nearly ran into her truck because she couldn't break away from his gaze to watch where she was going. Instinct saved her and she grabbed the door handle for support, stopping just in time.

Wondering how she would get through the morning, Sarah yanked the door open and escaped inside. The escape was short-lived, however, as Dan walked around the front of the vehicle and was soon sitting beside her. Her hands shook when she tried to start the engine, and she felt like a complete idiot.

And then a wave of indignation hit her, and her spine

straightened. She had absolutely no reason to feel embarrassed by Betty and Tom's behavior; nor had she any reason to fear the look in Dan's eyes. Disaster? What could possibly be disastrous about giving a client a tour of the nursery; and if she enjoyed a little male attention along the way—well, that wasn't disastrous either! She was thirty-one years old and a widow, and it was absurd for those two to make her feel like a guilty teenager. But, then, she loved them both too much to feel angry. Instead she smiled, and the smile turned into a soft chuckle. She glanced over at Dan and saw that he was barely suppressing his own laughter.

"What happens," he asked, "when a little girl grows up and becomes the boss?"

Sarah gave him a woeful look and replied, "Obviously, there are ways in which a little girl never grows up."

"Well, she looks quite grown up to me. In fact," he said, his dark brows arching upward, "she looks quite lovely this morning."

"Why, thank you," Sarah replied smoothly. "It's nice to hear that somebody approves. I've had far too much good advice for one day."

"I promise not to offer you a single piece of it," he swore, raising his hand in a scout salute. "Now, where are these roses I came to see?"

Sarah started the pickup and pulled out of the lot onto the dirt road that ran back into the nursery property. "I'm saving the roses for later," she said. "We're going to start on the western boundary line with the ornamental plums, cherries, and pears."

And so the morning passed with Dan Lowell getting an education in tree identification, nursery management, and insect control. Sarah walked him through rows of mountain ash and all varieties of hemlock and spruce. He was overwhelmed by the dawn redwoods and thought the mimosa, though still not quite ready to bloom, looked like something out of Disney's *Fantasia,* all lined up in a row to dance a ballet. Sarah also showed him some rare specimens imported from China, the names of which he promptly forgot or couldn't pronounce. They reached the rhododendrons, azaleas, and lilacs at about eleven-thirty. Then Sarah showed him her favorite shrubs, the camellias, which were kept protected from bitter cold by rows of spruce planted between and around the bushes. Next they saw the dogwoods, including a rare fragrant variety, the four-inch blooms of which Sarah had to describe, since the plants had finished their flowering cycle. Then they headed for the rose fields.

It had been a wonderful morning, and Sarah had learned quickly why Dan was such an extraordinarily successful businessman. His enthusiasm was infectious; it poured out of him in great waves, and it was impossible not to be caught up in it. He wanted to know everything and would listen to the driest details with rapt attention. Sarah could almost see him assessing and filing the information. His questions were astute and took into account all information previously given. By the time they drove up to the roses and began their tour, Sarah fully expected to be asked for a complete genealogy of each rose and a full description of her grafting methods for hybrid teas and tree roses.

She wasn't far off the mark.

"Now, this is one of my mistakes," she said stopping to point out a row of white roses just beginning to bloom.

Dan cast a critical eye down the row. "Their stems are too weak. Right?"

She nodded. "And the bud isn't consistently well formed. It opens to a rather nice flower"— she pointed out one fully opened bloom—"but then the stems droop."

"What will you do with it?" Dan asked. "It seems a shame to throw the whole thing out because of a skimpy stem and a disappointing bud."

"Oh, I'll keep working at it," Sarah assured him. "White roses are hard. There aren't many really nice ones. They also attract lots of insects, and the average gardener considers them a bother."

"So you're going to make one that's worth the effort."

It wasn't a question, and Sarah didn't deny it. Instead, she smiled her agreement.

"You realize I'd like to take the lot of them an move them about four miles in that direction." Dan waved his arm toward the southeast.

Sarah shrugged. "Except for the experimentals, they're all for sale."

"In fact," Dan continued thoughtfully, as though he hadn't heard her speak, "I'd like to take everything I've seen this morning and move it over there . . . Sarah?" He turned quickly to look at her, and there was a gleam of excitement in his eye. "Why not?" he said simply.

"Why not what?" Sarah looked at him, puzzled.

"Why not move it all?"

He's really crazy, she thought to herself. *I'm being led around by the nose by a charmingly eccentric nut.*

"I'm sorry," she said finally with a shake of her blond head. "I knew I should've worn my hat. The sun's getting to me. I could have sworn you just suggested moving the entire stock of Ashcroft Nursery to your property."

"I did." Dan smiled.

She stared at him, then said the first thing that came to her. "You're out of your mind."

"You're beautiful."

"I think I'd better sit down."

Very slowly, not for a minute thinking she could take him seriously—in any regard—Sarah walked back toward the truck. She'd gotten about halfway there when she stopped short and asked, "Do you have any idea what you're saying? Ashcroft is not a wholesale nursery, Dan. We ship roses all over the country by mail order, and we sell the nursery stock to retail customers who come in looking for interesting specimens to liven up their yards. Some of the trees you saw this morning are twenty years old; some even older. It's an incredible job to move a twenty- or twenty-five-foot tree, and it can cost thousands of dollars—just for one of them!"

"So?" was his nonplussed reply to her little speech.

"'So?'!" Sarah squeaked in shock. "It would cost

hundreds of thousands—no, millions!—to buy and move all of my stock. You can't be seriously considering it!"

"I've already considered it," he replied. "It's a wonderful idea—the work of a true visionary." Dan grinned unabashedly.

"Maybe several nice specimens here and there . . . in your own yard, perhaps. But not *all* of them!"

"All of them." He nodded briskly. "I want you to landscape the entire place. Oh, I'll have to convince my planning committee." His careless shrug told her how seriously he took that venerable body. "They'll fuss about the budget and insist we can't afford it. But it's not really a problem."

He said it with such assurance that Sarah almost believed he meant it. Still, the whole idea was preposterous. Surely it was just an impulsive suggestion on his part. Soon he'd reconsider and decide that white pine and sea-green juniper would do just fine. A couple of yew here and there . . . Yes, that was more like it.

"We'll have to talk about this," she said cautiously and once more began walking toward the truck. When she realized Dan wasn't following, she turned and looked back. He had stopped at the end of a row of roses and was standing with one hand cupped under a deep red bloom. The look on his face was odd, Sarah thought. Something like awe and longing and sadness all mixed together.

There was something about that look that touched her deeply. They'd been talking nearly nonstop, and he'd been full of enthusiasm all morning. He'd just made an outrageously impulsive decision that she suspected was based more on enthusiasm than good sense. And yet, now his face told her that there was something else here that she wasn't seeing—something below the surface charm. Whatever it was, it sparked something at once hopeful and poignant inside her. Without examining her reasons, Sarah made an impulsive decision of her own.

They'd come to the end of the tour; it was lunchtime, and the sun overhead was hot. They should be heading back to the office, but she wasn't ready for the morning to end—and neither, apparently, was Dan.

"I've got one more thing to show you," said Sarah when Dan finally joined her.

"Have you saved the best for last?"

"Of course," she said, and smiled a tiny, secretive smile. "But it's not for sale."

The pickup rolled to a stop in the far southeastern corner of the Ashcroft property. There was no nursery stock planted there. Only the natural landscape of the Maryland woods, slightly cleared to allow for the thick, green growth of grass, surrounded them. Before them was a tall, white wooden gate that marked the only break in a thick twelve-foot-high wall of dark red brick.

"What's in there?" Dan asked.

"You'll see," Sarah replied. "Before we go in, I thought you might like to know we've reached the end of my property and the beginning of yours. Those woods over there"—she pointed—"belong to you."

Dan looked interested. "Yes, I thought those trees looked familiar."

"Well, I hope those trees will continue to look familiar. I've had nightmares wondering what you were planning for this little corner of your world."

"How about a grocery store parking lot?" he asked innocently.

"If you're serious," Sarah warned, "I may move to Florida and take all my roses with me."

"Lord!" he exclaimed. "What do you suggest, then?"

She pursed her lips thoughtfully. "How about a cemetery?"

"Um, right!" Dan coughed discreetly and added, "Every town should have one."

Sarah chuckled and got out to lead the way up to the tall white gate. Once there, she reached for the latch and pushed the gate open; then she stood back and bade Dan enter before her. She smiled at his wary expression and followed him in, closing the gate behind her quietly.

For a long time they stood without speaking. Then, slowly, Dan began to walk around the flagstone path of the enclosure. Sarah followed.

She knew intuitively that the time for lectures had passed. He didn't care that he'd stopped to look at a Charles de Mills rose of the *gallica* classification, which bloomed in colors ranging from rose pink to deep lavender. Nor did he want to know that the light crimson blooms with the intense perfume he was smelling were *Rosa gallica officinalis,* or Apothecary Rose, which was considered to be the Adam of all European roses. And it was certainly not the time for an accounting of the begat's. *Rosa gallica* crossed with *Rosa moschata* begat the Autumn Damask, and when it was crossed with *Rosa canina,* it begat the *alba.* But when it was crossed with *Rosa phoenicia*, it begat the Damask. No, this was not the time.

Sarah watched the expression on Dan's face as he turned from time to time, and she was fully conscious of what he must be experiencing. She let the spell of the place take her as well, as it always did. They continued in silence, leaving the path that went around the perimeter of the garden to wander the smaller paths that wound among open beds. Here there were other plants: A few late-blooming daffodils still graced the lush green grass with splashes of yellow; holly, hemlock, and low spreading juniper provided an occasional spot of evergreen to take the garden through the barren winter months. For height and graceful form, several red dogwoods were scattered randomly over the grassy plots. And one old, gnarled crab apple tree dominated the exact center of the large, rectangular-shaped enclosure.

Mostly, though, there were roses—dozens and dozens of roses—some just budding up from dormancy, some actually finished with their early spring blooming, and others in full, splendid color, heavily laden with blossoms of every imaginable shade. Blood red, deep russet, coral pink, lavender, and all shades of white from blushing ivory to pure, clean snow. And the smells—

oh, yes, the smells were intoxicating; from heavy damask to light musk, the heady fragrances mingled together and wafted through the warm air.

Sarah and Dan had walked about halfway around the high-walled garden when he stopped and turned, as though he'd only just remembered she was there. All of the arrogance was gone from his expression. The look that now touched those crystal blue eyes spoke of wonderment and awe.

"Sarah . . ." he breathed almost reverently, "this is . . ."— his gaze cast around, searching—". . . unearthly."

Sarah's lips wore a satisfied smile, the one that always stole over her when she gazed upon her enchanted and private world. They began walking once more, and this time Sarah kept apace of him.

"My father and I planted this garden," she told him. "I was five, and he told me the story of each rose as we planted it. Such wonderful stories! I learned all my ancient history then—tales of knights in armor, unrequited love, wars fought for honor and passion . . . I can never think of my father without thinking of this garden. It's like . . . like he's still here, watching over the place"— she shrugged—"watching over all of Ashcroft, really, but I feel him here most strongly. It's odd, too, because the trees were his real passion, not the roses."

Sarah reached out and plucked a spent blossom from a Rose du Roi bush, fingering the velvety bright red petals thoughtfully. They began walking again, and this time Sarah was pensive. She had spoken of her father, but she was thinking more of the man who walked beside her. She was glad she had brought Dan here. Why did she feel an overwhelming urge to share this intimate part of herself with him? His manner, his look—everything about him—inspired such intimacy. He was warm, open, inviting—he was, in a word, charismatic. She was drawn to him in a way that both excited and frightened her; yet, here, in her garden, fear was impossible.

Sarah and Dan came to a halt near the center of the garden. Dan was still looking about him as though it were all a mirage that would disappear if he closed his eyes for even a second. Sarah laughed softly at his look of unveiled wonder, glad of her decision to share her special place with him.

She decided to risk a bit more. Impulsively, she reached out to take his hand, pouring the petals she held into his palm and closing his fingers around them. The intense damask fragrance wafted between them. Then, with a hesitant smile, she walked a few feet off the path across the grass and seated herself on the wooden bench in the center of the garden under the huge old crab apple tree. Looking back at Dan, she patted the spot beside her.

Dan glanced from Sarah to the petals in his hand and then back to her once more. His eyes never left hers as he walked toward the bench and then, finally, obeyed her unspoken request.

"Your father was a very special man," he said at last in a strangely husky voice.

Sarah nodded. "He was. He was no businessman; thank God for Henry Turner, or we probably would have lost the nursery years ago. All Daddy cared about were his trees and his roses. He gave me this garden for my own. And he made it very clear that no one else was to come here but me and whomever I invited. Even he asked permission to come do the upkeep. There were many people on the rest of the property—gardeners, customers, the moving crews—but this garden was always off limits."

"And did you find much need for such solitude?" Dan asked, his blue eyes now focused on her instead of their surroundings.

Sarah looked out over the garden. "There was enough," she said simply. And she thought about how there had been even more need in her adult life than there had been as a child. Somehow, the old taboo had lasted even when her father had died; Bill had never set foot in her garden. She'd always had a place to go when things became too much to bear.

Dan studied her profile carefully and said, "I have the

feeling there were far too many occasions for you to need this garden, but I'm glad it was here, all the same."

Taken off guard—had her thoughts had been so transparent?—Sarah looked at him, startled. His look invited her to continue, but she wasn't ready to share those feelings. She'd gone as far as she could.

Instead of pushing her to say more, Dan spoke of his own thoughts. "There were a lot of times I wished I'd had a place like this to come to." He gestured at the wild profusion of color around him. "In a way, I guess I have. He smiled. "My mother grew roses."

"Oh?" Sarah looked at him curiously, hoping he'd tell her why her own favorite flower was obviously his— and perhaps what the sad look she'd noted earlier was all about.

"She had nothing like this, of course." He shrugged. "There was only room for a couple of tubs in our otherwise concrete backyard. But they grew for her. I remember their being a bud or two on our kitchen windowsill from spring through fall, as long as she was alive."

Sarah stared at his handsome profile and listened as he talked. Everything was perfectly still—hot, hazy, timeless. Dan's voice was soft, mellow, and blurred around the edges of his words. Sarah felt those words melting into the heavily scented summerlike air until they became a part of the color and the fragrance and the stillness. Entrancing. Beguiling. Lovely.

"My mother was like your father, I suppose," Dan continued. "She understood the importance of beauty in a world that was full of so much ugliness. She made up stories for my two brothers and me—stories about leprechauns and fairies that lived under her roses. And we absolutely believed that such things could happen, even in the middle of all that concrete. Even though, on the other side of our fence, people were . . . well, even though things could be wretched. Mama used to say that every bud she could coax into bloom was another dream come true. She'd brought the cuttings from Ireland, and as long as they were alive, she said, so were the dreams she'd brought with her."

When he stopped speaking, Sarah held her breath. The anticipation of hearing him finish what he'd started was almost painful. At last, she had to ask, "And did her dreams come true?"

Dan sighed. "I don't know. I was never quite sure what they were. But, somehow, I don't think so. She lost one son to Vietnam, and my father died in a factory accident not long after. She died the year I finished college. Perhaps if she'd know that I . . . that I managed to make my way . . ."

Without stopping to think, Sarah put her hand over his hand as it clutched the rose petals. "I can't imagine she ever had a moment's doubt about you."

Dan's head jerked around to meet her gaze. For a minute he let her see the doubt and pain in his eyes, and then his look changed. Slowly, he smiled. "Yes, she had that kind of implicit faith in the future."

Sarah returned his smile. "And you don't?"

He tilted his dark head thoughtfully. It was getting to be a familiar gesture to Sarah. "It's different. Mine is a more calculated faith."

Sarah laughed softly. "You mean you rely on your wits to get what you want, and not on fate?"

Dan grinned. "My father wasn't quite the optimist that Mother was. I learned a few things from him, too, I guess."

"Where are your mother's roses now?" she asked. "Do you still have them?"

He shook his head sadly. "I tried for the longest time to keep them alive, but they were determined to die. But do you know"—he turned his gaze back to hers for a moment—"seeing this place has made me realize that I never really lost those few scraggly bushes. They're just as alive as they ever were. All the time I've been living the life of a calculating businessman, I was actually carrying a bit of my mother's roses with me." He glanced down at Sarah's hand, which still covered his fist, and slowly his hand turned and opened until their fingers were intertwined, the petals of the rose pressed between their palms.

His eyes raised to meet hers. "Sarah . . . thanks for showing me your garden. You've given me something very special."

Her instinct was to draw back, to brush off the moment with something meaningless, like "You're quite welcome." She wanted to pull away from the intimacy that was rapidly overtaking anything in her experience and threatening to overwhelm her with its potent force. It had been coming all morning—had been hovering in the air the day before—and it was much, much too soon.

But she couldn't do it. She couldn't crush the moment for him, even if it terrified her to let this happen. After all, that was what her garden was for—special times, deep thoughts, secrets shared with only the flowers and the birds and the sky. That he was sharing his soul with her was too special a gift to throw back at him.

And as she hesitated she saw his look change. The past was rapidly fading away and they were both right there, alone with the heat and the sunshine and the roses.

Dan's gaze raked over her features—searching, intently questioning, stripping away whatever defense she considered making. Desire flickered in his ice-blue look. Sarah's features softened and her lower lip quivered slightly; her whole body felt the force of the shimmering heat in the air between them.

"Sarah . . ." Dan's free hand reached out quickly as though he would grab both her and the moment before both fled. He cupped her face, his thumb tracing a line across her mouth. Her lips parted slightly and her eyes widened as she realized the inevitability of what was going to happen. His eyes told her she had no choice— that neither of them had a choice anymore—and they begged her at the same time not to be frightened. Her emerald gaze and his blue one locked as Dan pulled their joined hands out from between them and slowly leaned toward her. Sarah felt his warm breath on her cheek—

watched the blue of his eyes even when she couldn't see him clearly anymore; finally the scent of his cologne was close enough to overshadow even the heavy damask around them. When his lips brushed hers lightly, she let go of his hand to touch his shoulder, and his freed hand quickly laced through the honey silk of her hair to pull her mouth against his. The petals they'd been holding floated to the ground, forgotten.

Never too fast, never for a moment losing any of that sense of timelessness that had been with them since entering the garden, Dan melded his lips to hers with the same intensity as the pulsing waves between them— growing, testing, anticipating. Not once did he spoil it by trying to move too fast or by sacrificing sensuality for technique, instinct for expertise. Every persuasive touch of his mouth against hers said that he wanted her there with him, that it was something they were discovering together. And Sarah never considered not answering him with her own trembling lips.

When Dan pulled back, Sarah heard herself whimper softly, and with her eyes still closed she drew a ragged breath to steady her pounding heart.

"Sarah?"

Her name was a whispered caress carried on the warm breeze. Slowly, she opened her eyes to meet Dan's eyes, only inches from her own. She found her feelings of arousal and wonderment mirrored in his open, vulnerable look, and the look was as bewitching as the kiss had been.

"Sarah," he whispered again, and hesitantly, almost as though he were afraid of what he would find, he leaned toward her once more.

The hesitation fled with the first touch of his mouth against hers. Then his arms slid around her and she melted against him. Deeper and deeper they drank from the well of sensations newly discovered. Bolder and bolder the kiss became until Dan was clutching her tightly in his arms and groaning deeply in his chest as Sarah nearly gasped for breath.

Suddenly, Sarah realized he was pulling her to her feet, and she was pressed against his hard body. Her feet barely touched the ground. The passion that had begun with the mere touch of their lips now engulfed their entire beings. She felt herself shaking as her breasts were crushed against his chest. His thighs trembled where they met hers, and the taut evidence of his masculinity stirred against the yielding softness of her belly. Compulsively, Sarah sought to hold him closer and heard him breathe raspingly.

I'm going to let this man make love to me, she thought mindlessly. *Right here . . . right now.* And the truth was a stunning blow.

Abruptly, Sarah tore her mouth from Dan's and gulped, pushing weakly at his shoulders with shaking hands. "Dan! We've got . . . to stop." It was all she could manage between gasps for air. "Please!"

Sarah was eternally grateful when, with a soul-wrenching groan, Dan did stop trying to kiss her. He held her tightly, though, one large hand keeping her head buried against his neck. "Why?" he whispered. "Why do we have to stop? Sarah . . ."

"I . . . I can't," she said brokenly. "It's . . . I just can't." The words sounded trite and harsh to her own ears, but she had to say them. She was appalled with herself and could only wonder if she'd left her good sense on the other side of the closed white gate. What was she doing in the arms of a man who was, for all intents and purposes, a stranger? Had she become that lonely? She shivered as she acknowledged that, stranger or not, Dan had just elicited more passion from her with a single kiss than she'd felt in all of her marriage. Worst of all, he was a client: He'd come to buy roses. The danger signs were fully lit now; business and pleasure didn't mix. But oh, how well Dan Lowell mixed them!

Dan's breathing was still ragged as he continued to hold her in his arms. She didn't try to move away but remained very still, allowing the passion they'd built to die down from its white heat, although she knew it could

easily have blazed again with very little encouragement.
Finally, his arms loosened their embrace and his hand
fell away from her head. She leaned back a little and
risked meeting his gaze.

"I'm . . . I'm sorry," she said quietly.

"I'm not," he replied with a shake of his head and an
expression that reminded Sarah of the one he'd worn
when he'd first seen the rose garden. He was as shocked
and as moved by what had happened as she. "I'm not at
all sorry," he continued. "I only wish you hadn't stopped.
But"—he smiled a little—"I understand. I'm not a patient man, Sarah Turner. I'm used to taking what I want,
and it's new for me to want something that requires
another party's consent for it to be worth having." He
stopped a little way back from her, keeping his hands
on her shoulders, and his eyes, filled with longing and
a hint of that passion Sarah had just tasted, roamed over
her.

"I want you," he said in that same mellow, beguiling
voice that melted Sarah right to the bone. "If I have to
give you time, I will—somehow."

Sarah stared at him. There was no possibility she could
misunderstand. He would give her time, but he intended
to make love to her. And how, Sarah thought, could she
ever convincingly deny that she wanted him, too? It was
absurd! They were strangers, weren't they? Well, weren't
they?

When Sarah couldn't return his gaze any longer, she
turned away, saying, "I should be getting back to the
office."

Dan hesitated, then chuckled softly. "All right. I'll
let you off the hook this time. Back to business. When
can you have the figures ready for the landscaping contract?"

They walked back to the gate. Sarah stopped short,
shaking her head a little at his abrupt change of mood
and subject. "You're actually serious about that?" she
asked, still a bit disconcerted. "You want me to draw up
a proposal?"

"Of course I'm serious," Dan replied. "What does it take to convince you? I've never had to talk anyone into selling me merchandise." He took her elbow and steered her through the gate. "How can I talk sensibly to my planning committee if I don't have facts and figures? They're quite insistent on that, unfortunately."

Sarah chuckled pityingly. "Poor thing. What makes you think they'll agree to giving the landscaping contract to a retail nursery?"

Dan gave her a winning look. "I'll persuade them."

She raised one brow and drew back to look at him skeptically.

They had reached the pickup, and as Dan held the driver's door open for her he said, "Trust me. Your magnificent plants will soon be gracing the manicured grounds of . . . of Rosecroft. There! You see? It's kismet. I've been holding off on naming the place, and now I know why. I had to come see your roses. Rosecroft. It's perfect, don't you think?" He turned to the closed white gate of the garden they'd just left, and then he looked back at Sarah. His eyes lingered on her amazed expression, watched her lips for a long while, and then he smiled tenderly.

Sarah was trembling, although she couldn't tell if it was from passion or excitement from the prospect of the contract that Dan was proposing. Both, probably. "I . . . I love it," she said honestly. And suddenly she wanted with all her heart for the project to work—for his sake as well as her own. It seemed so very important to him. Still, she didn't dare let herself believe that it could actually work.

"It will take some time to draw up the proposal," she said as Dan walked around to climb in the passenger side of the truck beside her.

"How long?"

"Well, if I had an aerial photograph and maps of the completed town—an artist's map and one that shows sewer, gas, electric, and phone lines would be ideal— perhaps I could put something together in, say, a week?"

"I've got the maps in my car. How about Friday?"

"Friday?" Sarah nearly stalled the truck at the staggering thought of having to compile all the necessary information in three days.

"That's as long as I think I can wait to see you again," he explained brightly. "Have dinner with me and I'll give you until dessert to have me panting all over again for Peace roses and dawn redwoods."

Sarah glanced at him sideways. "Are you or are you not proposing a business meeting?" she asked suspiciously.

"I told you," he answered, "you've got until dessert."

When Sarah walked into the nursery office a few minutes after saying good-bye to Dan, her expression was pensive.

"I was about to send Tom out to look for you," Betty remarked, looking up as Sarah entered. "What happened? Does he want to buy anything?"

"Roses..." Sarah said softly, looking down at the maps in her hand. "He mostly wants roses." She stopped in the middle of the room and frowned. Was that true? Did he mostly want roses—or did he want *her*?

"From the look on your face, he isn't the only one doing the wanting!" Betty turned back to her work with a disgusted "Hmph."

"Oh, Betts," Sarah scoffed, "I'm thirty-one years old, for heaven's sake. I wish you wouldn't treat me like a child!" And she shut the door of her office to ward off further comment.

"You may be thirty-one," Betty muttered, "but right now you look like you're sixteen and have just been kissed for the first time."

- 3 -

FOR THE FOLLOWING three days, Sarah turned nursery operations over to Betty and Tom while she sequestered herself in her office to work on the landscape proposal for LINC's new town, Rosecroft. Over and over again she had to struggle to take the project seriously. She still couldn't believe any sane planning committee would approve the cost, and she listened constantly for the phone to ring, expecting Dan to call and say he'd had second thoughts. Several times she was ready to give up the whole thing as sheer folly, and then her eyes came to rest on the stack of equipment repair orders, the cost estimates for installing the new heating system in the greenhouses, and the operating budget for the following year.

The prospects were simply too tantalizing to resist. If she sold all her stock, she would have the money and the space—and the time—to set up her hybridization research. And she'd have the time to do something with

41

her life besides work! Therefore, Sarah applied herself
to the task day and night until Friday at six o'clock, when
she threw down her pen and flopped back in the chair
behind her desk to groan in satisfied relief.

It was outrageous. She hadn't tried to cut the cost;
she had only given Dan the best price she could reason-
ably afford—and it was still outrageous. But it was also
done.

Glancing at her watch, Sarah hurriedly stacked the
final ledger sheet, the architectural plans, and the written
proposal and shoved it all into her infrequently used
briefcase.

Twenty minutes later, she was soaking in a bubble
bath and wondering where Dan would take her to eat.
Nothing too intimate, she hoped; after all, they were
going to talk business...weren't they? Yes, dammit,
they were!

When she'd finished applying her makeup, Sarah cast
a critical eye at her appearance. Deep-green irises ringed
in black with thick lashes several shades darker than her
warm blond hair stared back at her. Her eyes were her
best feature—no doubt about it. She was more critical
of her mouth, which she thought entirely too small, and
her too-pale skin blushed more easily than she would
have liked. Ignoring the heat and humidity, she'd chosen
to leave her hair down, and now its gentle waves lay
shining around her shoulders in a golden cloud.

Sarah unwound the towel from her slender body and
went to her wardrobe, where she spent ten minutes deciding what to wear. All of her proper-looking suits she
discarded as either too old, too frumpy or too...well,
just *too*. And it was seven-twenty when she pulled out
an Oriental-style sleeveless dress with a high Mandarin
collar. The teal-blue silk fitted her body, emphasizing
her gentle curves, and was, Sarah thought, altogether
elegant. She hurriedly looked for her shoes and handbag,
and as she was buckling the ankle straps of her heels,
she heard a car door slam in the driveway. As an after-
thought she sprayed a generous dose of her favorite co-

logne in the general direction of her neck and shoulders, and was just closing her bedroom window against the ever-present threat of a thunderstorm, when the knock at the screen door came.

"I'll be right down, Dan!" she called. "Come on in." She grabbed her clutch bag and was about to hurry down the stairs when she caught a glimpse of herself in the mirror. She paused, certain that something was missing. "Oh, damn," she swore softly, and dropped the purse in order to rummage through her jewelry box. By the time she actually left the room, she was wearing a wide gold and blue enamel bracelet inlaid with mother-of-pearl, and matching loop earrings.

When Sarah arrived at the bottom of the stairs, her cheeks were flushed and her eyes bright; she hardly recognized herself. A warning voice in her head told her to slow down, and she reminded herself that she would have to adopt an entirely businesslike attitude for the evening. If she were having a hard time convincing herself of that, it would be impossible to convince Dan.

She found him sitting on the porch swing, waiting for her. Immediately, all thoughts of business fled. Dan ceased to be the head of Lowell Industrial Corporation and became, very simply, the sexiest man she'd ever seen—and her date for the evening. He wore dark chocolate-colored slacks and a jacket the color of warm, rich cream. His shirt was also cream-colored and, like the other she'd seen him wear, was tailored to emphasize his narrow waist and broad shoulders. He wore his clothing with casual sophistication and an unapologetic arrogance about the devastatingly male picture he made. His arms were draped negligently over the back of the swing, and his legs were stretched out before him, crossed at the ankle. As she watched him his eyes raked her from head to toe almost insolently.

"Did it occur to you when you hollered at me to come in that it could have been a mad rapist knocking?" The question was asked with apparent indifference.

Sarah blinked in confusion. "Do rapists usually knock?"

she asked, her eyes wide with not-altogether-feigned innocence.

"Normally *I* wouldn't," he answered with a shrug, "but I'll have to make an exception if you don't stop looking at me like that."

His words were like a splash of ice water and served to remind her as nothing she'd told herself had that this was to be a business meeting.

"As I recall," Sarah began sweetly, "you asked me to dinner so I could present my proposal for landscaping your new town. I've spent every waking hour of the last three days preparing the proposal, and it's very likely that what you are seeing in my eyes is either exhaustion or starvation or both. Shall we go?"

Dan grinned, and the tension was broken. "So you took it seriously? Good." He got up to take her arm and steer her down the steps toward his car. He'd taken her briefcase from her and tossed it behind the passenger's seat of his two-seater Mercedes. Sarah was about to get in when his hand on her arm stopped her. She looked at him questioningly.

"You look beautiful, Sarah," he said huskily. "It's probably exhaustion or starvation you see in my eyes, too, because I haven't been able to sleep or eat, thinking about being with you tonight. I'll try to behave, but don't expect miracles. And anyway," he added with a slow smile, "I only gave you until dessert. After that, business is over."

"Do you turn mad rapist before or after the last mouthful of chocolate mousse?" she asked in dead seriousness, and then slid into the passenger seat without waiting for his reply.

Dan chuckled and closed the door.

They'd been driving down Route 97 toward Washington, D.C. for ten minutes when Sarah asked, "Where are we going?"

"I found the perfect spot," Dan replied with assurance. "Unless you had someplace special in mind?"

"No," Sarah replied, relieved that she didn't have to

make the choice. He was new to her city, and it wouldn't have been a surprise if he'd asked her advice in the matter. Still, she'd not had much opportunity to sample the finer restaurants of Washington and knew only names and reputations.

Dan swore often and vehemently at the Friday-night traffic on the Capital Beltway and on Wisconsin Avenue leading into the District. Sarah had to suppress a chuckle. Driving in Washington was never easy, but she thought that for someone accustomed to New York City traffic, it shouldn't be that difficult.

"Do you always enjoy driving so much?" she asked once after a particularly hair-raising turn around a complicated traffic circle.

"What?" Dan glanced at her with a scowl, but seeing the look on her face, his scowl disappeared and was replaced by a crooked smile. In New York I take taxis— when I'm not being chauffered. Sometimes I miss the simple things, like driving. I wouldn't mind if I were better at it, though. I just wish Joan had found me a place to live closer to Rosecroft—but then, our offices will be in the District for a while."

Sarah noted how smoothly the name *Rosecroft* slipped off his tongue, as though he'd been calling it that for years. "So you're living in the District?" she asked. "Where?"

"Oh, well, it's a rather nice place, actually. Joan, my secretary, is good at picking them . . . Ah! Here we are." Dan executed an amazing turn and they came to an abrupt halt.

She looked out the window in time to have the door opened for her by a formally attired valet. The doorman helped her out of the car, and she threw a startled look at Dan as he joined her. The car disappeared, presumably spirited away by another white-gloved attendant.

"This is the Ritz-Carlton," Sarah pointed out unnecessarily as Dan took her elbow and guided her toward the door of the very exclusive hotel.

"Yes, I know," he answered smoothly.

"Have you eaten at the Jockey Club?" she asked, knowing that the restaurant was supposed to be one of D.C.'s very finest. Actually, it was one of the few in which she'd eaten herself. And she knew very well it was not the place to hold a business meeting.

"The dining room is excellent," said Dan in answer to her question as he ushered her up the flight of wide, Carrara marble stairs that led to the lobby.

Sarah looked at her surroundings appreciatively. The lobby was small and beautifully appointed in the Georgian style. Like the rest of the hotel, it was warm and intimate and had the feel of an elegant private home. The furnishings were antiques or reproductions; the carpets were Oriental. Sarah noted the entrance to the dining room on the left. When Dan turned to the right instead, she looked up at him, puzzled.

"I thought our business would be better conducted in private this evening," he replied to her unspoken question as they stopped in front of the elevator.

And then the truth hit her: "You're living here, aren't you?"

"Hmm," he replied affirmatively, guiding her into the elevator.

Sarah nearly balked, feeling very much as though they were playing the spider and the fly. She glanced sideways at Dan. His potent male charm, the masculine smell of him, the possessive way he looked at her, and the light, caressing way he touched her hand, her arm, her waist, at the slightest provocation—these were the bait he was using to capture her. And for the life of her, she couldn't think of a good reason not to let him ... except that she had a strong feeling that, once caught, she'd never be free again. Yes, having felt the force of his kiss, she was certain his bite was deadly.

The ride up the elevator to the eighth floor was too short for Sarah to sort out her ambivalent feelings; and too quickly she found herself standing before the dark-paneled door to Dan's suite. And then she was standing in the living room and he was turning on lights that cast a warm, mellow glow around the high-ceilinged, spacious room. She was surrounded by exquisite antiques and more Oriental rugs covering highly polished oak floors. Everywhere she looked there was wood and brass. The paintings on the vanilla-colored walls were originals, and she recognized a watercolor by one of her favorite artists. The place effused elegance, quality, class—and intimacy. And Sarah loved it.

Behind her, Dan had picked up the phone from a table just inside the door and was making arrangements for their dinner. Well, at least, the spider was planning to serve the fly a last meal, she thought dryly.

Stop it, she told herself. *He's behaved like a perfect gentleman—and how can anyone staying at a hotel like this be anything less than a gentleman?* She knew that if she spent any more time worrying that he would turn into the mad rapist he'd jokingly alluded to being, she'd never be able to present the proposal effectively. Somehow, she had to get her mind off the fact that she was in the hotel suite of a very attractive man—one who'd made no secret of the fact that he wanted to make love to her—and put her attention on the business of selling Ashcroft Nursery stock to Lowell Industrial Corporation. She turned from her perusal of the living room to look at Dan. She tried to think of him as the president and chairman of the board of one of the major land-developing corporations in the country instead of . . . instead of a man?

She sighed. The task was hopeless.

"Yes, Claude," Dan was saying, "we'd like dinner in half an hour . . . Yes, that'll be fine." He replaced the receiver, looked up at her with a grin, and asked, "Now, what will you have to drink?" He walked across the room to a small marble-topped table that served as a bar.

Sarah turned to look out one of the windows. "Gin and tonic, please," she replied cautiously. She didn't drink alcohol often and hoped he mixed a weak drink. She wanted her wits about her.

Dan brought the glass to her and they talked—harm-

lessly enough—about the view of Massachusetts Avenue
from the room. Sarah pointed out he Indonesian Embassy
across the street. Dan said he'd been jogging in the park
next to it. Sarah told him about the Society of the Cin-
cinnati Museum next door to the hotel, which was full
of memorabilia of that famous battleship. Dan was delighted to discover that Sarah was an avid sightseer and
museum-goer, and he made her promise to take him on
a tour of the nation's capital.

"I'm sure you've noticed all the embassies along Mass.
Avenue," Sarah remarked. "This is embassy row, and
it's one of my favorite streets in D.C. Of course, there
are no buildings in the District highter than the Capital,
so I can't give you a tour from the window, the way one
might from a New York high-rise."

Dan reached over and took the glass from her hand
and set it alongside his on a table beneath the window
as she continued. She drew in a sharp breath.

"Now, if you were staying at the Hay-Adams, you'd
be overlooking the White House. But then you wouldn't
have the park and it would be a longer drive," she stammered.

"Sarah . . ."

"And this place is so lovely . . ." she continued as he
turned her around to face him.

"Sarah, I want to kiss you." His face drew near hers,
and his mouth would have found its mark if she hadn't
turned her head, looking down as she did so.

"Dan . . . no." It was going to be impossible to refuse
if he persisted, and she knew it.

"Why not?" he asked softly, reaching up with one
hand to capture her chin and hold her head still. His lips
brushed hers lightly. "You're safe. Dinner will be here
soon."

"No . . . I don't want you to," she murmured weakly,
her fingers curling into her palms in an effort to keep
from touching him.

He drew back fractionally. His eyes held hers. "You
lie," he accused gently.

Sarah's eyes were wide and shining. She stared into the depths of his, which were sky blue, as he bowed his head once more, slowly, deliberately, until their lips touched. His hand moved to the nape of her neck and tilted her head to make the pressure of his mouth on hers more exact. Still, Sarah held her breath, unable to move, unable to break the contact between their eyes. But when his mouth moved against hers teasingly, persuasively, a tiny sound escaped her from deep in her throat. Her eyes closed and her hands came up to cling to his shoulders.

Dan's arms were around her instantly, holding her to him as though he had no intention of ever letting her go. Their mouths opened together, and at once they were transported back to that morning in the rose garden. Sarah felt herself drowning in wave after wave of unleashed passion.

"Oh, Sarah!" Dan whispered hoarsely against her cheek as his mouth found its way across her face to her ear and then down her neck. "Sarah, how can you lie about this?" His hands were everywhere, roaming boldly across her silk-covered hips and up her back. One hand held her to him as the other stretched across her ribs and then slid up to cup the underside of her breast. "I want you," he growled softly as his thumb traced a circle around the swelling peak, caressing the nipple so that it hardened and tingled deliciously. "Sarah," he whispered, "I want to look at you . . . touch you . . ."

Sarah moaned helplessly as he continued to tease the now throbbing bud through the fabric of her dress. Unable to stop herself she reached for his hand and pressed it fully against her, trying to ease some of the ache that was growing deep in her loins. All the while she knew she should be pushing his hand away. It was madness, and she would have to find a way to make them stop!

Dan reacted almost violently to her encouraging gesture, pulling her hips against his, the hardness of him cradled between the trembling softness of her thighs. "Sarah," he breathed, "when we make love, it's going to be like this. It's going to be good . . ."

Sarah's eyes flew open. Abruptly, she pulled her mouth away and pushed her hands against his chest.

"No!" he growled.

"Dan"—she swallowed his name with a gulp of air—"we have to stop now!"

"Why? Why do we have to stop, dammit?"

He was angry this time, and she couldn't blame him. They weren't teenagers necking at the drive-in. She had to lay down the ground rules or she'd be lost.

"I'm sorry," she began carefully, "but I'm not going to let this happen. You have to listen to me." She pushed again at his chest, her eyes closed tightly and her mouth set with a look of determination she didn't feel.

There was a long pause, and Sarah could feel his indecision in the shaking of his body. He was making a considerable effort to rein in on the feelings she'd allowed him to unleash. It stunned her to think a man could feel so ... so *strongly* about her. Bill never had ...

"All right," Dan said. "Tell me why it's not all right for two healthy adults who want each other to take what they want. This magic between us, Sarah, it's ..." Suddenly he released her, cutting his own words short.

Sarah breathed deeply—in relief?—and opened her eyes. "I'm not trying to be prudish," she said quietly. "And I truly don't want you to think I'm deliberately teasing you."

"I was beginning to wonder," he mumbled half angrily, turning away to reach for his glass of Scotch.

"Dan, it's very important to me that ... that whatever happens ..." Sarah took a deep breath and steadied herself, hating that it was so hard to make herself explain. "Whatever happens, it's very important to me that it not be mixed up with any business that we may transact. I've had some experience mixing business with ... sex." She whispered the word, shocked to the bone because she'd almost said *love*. That was insane. One didn't fall in love after two kisses, did one?

Dear God! She'd never been so confused!

"Are you trying to say," Dan began, a little less angrily

this time, "that you're afraid I'll mistake you for one of your damned trees?"

Sarah blushed and turned away to look out the window once more, her arms folded protectively over her middle. "I'm not going to try to explain it," she said flatly. "I'm not even going to pretend it makes sense. I'm a little confused right now, and perhaps it would be better if you just took me home and we conducted this meeting during regular hours at the nursery office."

His eyes narrowed as he studied her determine profile. "What happened to make you so scared?" he asked.

Sarah didn't blink, nor did she make any attempt to answer.

"So . . . you won't tell me why you're suddenly so terrified of me, but you still insist we play by your rules." He paused a moment. "What if I tell you to keep the damned trees—that I have no interest in them. Can I have you then?"

Sarah looked at him and studied the speculative light in his eyes. "But you do have an interest in our stock," she replied. "You've said you do, and if you change your mind now, you may change it again later." It felt very presumptuous, indeed, to be calling a man like Daniel Lowell capricious, but there was a great deal at stake here—on several different fronts. "I would rather have you make a decision once and for all, based on the facts. Then, at least, I'll know that the business arrangements are settled one way or the other."

"And then what?" he asked, calmly enough. When she didn't respond immediately, he nearly exploded. "Sarah! For God's sake, do you or do you not want to see me as a man and not a businessman?"

The look she gave him was at once pleading and wary. She was utterly miserable. It was a fair question, given what had transpired between them. It was a bloody awful question, given the length of time she'd known him. Yes, she wanted him—wanted him so badly, it terrified her. But no, she wasn't ready to commit herself to anything. It was the best she could do.

The look communicated itself to Dan and he sighed, the tension leaving his face. "All right, Sarah. I can see that doing it your way means I have to take it on blind faith that you'll let me know when you make up your mind. The problem is that I do want those damned trees. And the roses. And I don't see why I should give up either, them or you." Suddenly, he grinned disarmingly. "I have a problem. I want it all, and I'm never willing to settle for less if I think there's a snowball's chance in hell of getting everything."

He paused and frowned thoughtfully. Sarah didn't move. She held his gaze, her expression still one of wariness and determination.

"Here's what we'll do," Dan said, his expression brightening. "I'll make an agreement with you to buy every piece of stock Ashcroft has to sell. This is a verbal contract, and you can take me to court and win if I try to get out of it. How's that?"

Sarah gave him an astonished look. "You don't even know the price yet."

"I don't care about the price," he countered.

"But your planning committee will," she argued.

"If the cost goes over budget, I'll pay the difference personally."

Sarah hesitated, torn between wanting to have the matter settled and her need to keep this contract as formal and businesslike as possible. Slowly, she shook her head. "I want to show you the proposal. I worked hard on it, and I want to know that you understand exactly what I would do with your town and how much it would cost you."

Dan sighed resignedly. "Okay. I can see it's futile to argue. True, if I weren't so damned distracted by how much I want to make love to you, I'd be chomping at the bit to see what you've worked out."

Sarah smiled hesitantly. "Just think of me as a businesswoman."

Dan looked at her as though she'd lost her mind. "Let's try something easy, like...uh, swimming the English Channel. Come to think of it," he added, "that might help. At least the water's cold."

Sarah was saved further comment by a discreet knock at the door. Dinner was served, and Dan rose to the occasion by being the perfect host. The waiters came and went unobtrusively. Champagne was poured. The lobster was delicious. Everything was marvelous and elegant, and Sarah slowly relaxed as she realized that Dan was going to abide by the rules. They discussed nothing but business throughout the meal.

When the main course was removed and they had room on the table, Sarah opened her briefcase and spread before them an aerial map of the new town. Patiently, she identified the odd-looking inked stamps she'd made on the map, each representing some type of planting. Dan was not unfamiliar with a landscape architect's map, which made her work easier. The model city was large, and it hadn't been at all difficult to make use of her entire inventory of trees, shrubs, and roses. And although Ashcroft didn't sell seasonal bedding plants and bulbs, she'd planned space for them to be planted at the appropriate times. One nice feature of the land was that it was mostly wooded to begin with. Sarah had played on this, leaving some areas untouched altogether and others to be cleared only in the event of future building.

Even from the map she had been able to determine that her favorite spot in Rosecroft would be the open-air theater. She'd left the land around the coliseum-style arena partially wooded, adding flowering shrubs and an occasional unusual specimen from Ashcroft.

They were drinking brandy, their meal having been discreetly and efficiently spirited away, when she finished her presentation.

"And now we can look at the costs," she said, smiling at Dan, who sat across the table from her, paying rapt attention. In spite of his claim that he found her distracting, it hadn't ultimately taken much to shift his attention to the business at hand. Sarah could also see by the look in his eye that he was more than pleased with the proposal.

"One thing I don't understand," he said with a slight

frown. "Your degree is in horticulture and you specialize in hybridizing roses. Yet, this map was done by a landscape architect."

Sarah nodded. "Running the nursery means I have to be able to advise people on their landscaping needs. I have a certificate in landscape architecture in addition to my degree."

"But you don't like doing this sort of thing, do you?" he persisted.

Sarah lifted one shoulder in a tiny shrug. "It's not my field, no. I'd rather devote all my time to the roses, but I inherited a nursery complete with greenhouses, and in order to pay for my own habit"—she smiled—"I have to sell trees."

"What will you do when all those trees are here"— he gestured toward the map—"and you don't have to think about them anymore?"

"Plant roses," she answered unhesitatingly. "Perhaps we'll put in a few quick-selling items that turn a good profit."

"You aren't sentimentally attached to your father's view of what Ashcroft should be?"

"Not particularly," Sarah admitted. "I'd rather have the trees planted where they'll be enjoyed by everyone. Some of those trees are getting so large that in another couple of years, I wouldn't risk moving them. My father never intended to keep them, you know. Ashcroft *is* a nursery, not an arboretum, although it's becoming one. Daddy wouldn't have wanted that."

Dan paused before posing his next question. "Have you ever considered selling some land? Once the trees are gone, that would be fairly simple to do, I'd imagine."

The question caught her off guard. "Well, no, I've never thought about it," she replied. "The land has been in my family for generations. I wouldn't feel right selling it. Besides," she added, "I can use the space quite effectively. Just imagine all those empty fields filled with roses. If I sold any of it, I'd end up with housing developments crowding in around me." She shook her head. "No, thanks."

Dan grinned. "Is that another hint that I should watch what I put in the northwest corner of my town?"

Sarah sighed. "That cemetery sounded like a good idea to me. Much nicer than the town houses that you've got planned for it now."

"All right, Ms. Turner, let's see how much this thing is going to cost me—not that I'm overly concerned at this point. You present a very convincing argument, and I don't see how I'll ever be able to walk into my own office building and settle for anything but Chinese golden rain trees spilling their beautiful yellow petals all over the walk."

Sarah smiled serenely. "That's the whole idea."

In short order, the map was folded and put aside and the cost sheets were spread out for Dan's inspection. "So you'd do the landscaping yourself?" he asked, surprised. "Do you have the people and the equipment?"

"Not for anything this big," Sarah answered. "Tom and I would hire crews and train them. The cost figure here includes leasing the necessary equipment."

"This is a lot of money." He tapped one long finger on the final cost figure.

Sarah grinned. "Shocking, isn't it? I hate to say I told you so, *but* . . . Look on the bright side." She raised one brow suggestively. "You're getting a lot of trees."

"Are these prices the same you'd offer another client?"

She shrugged a little. "They're slightly less. An individual buying one tree pays one price, which includes moving and planting. Here I've cut the cost of the stock itself because you're paying a separate fee for labor."

"You aren't giving me a wholesale price on the stock?" he persisted.

"Is there any reason why I should?" she asked with a look that dared him to find one.

"No," he replied easily, "except that it's usually done that way."

"I told you," Sarah said evenly, "Ashcroft is a retail nursery. If you want wholesale, call Hank Tyler or Robert Barron. They'll give you all the white pine and eight-foot silver maples you could possibly want for a mere fraction of the price I've quoted you here. But"—she paused significantly—"don't expect to see any fifteen-foot golden-rain trees lining your office walk. And don't look for paperbark cherries outside of your window either. As for the bigleaf magnolias—the ones I showed you with the three-foot leaves and the ten-inch flowers? well, you can forget them altogether. And you will not be smelling the sweet smell of honeysuckle coming from your Heavenly Cloud flowering dogwoods in the spring."

Dan sighed, looked at her despairingly, and then smiled somewhat sheepishly. "You knew what you were doing when you insisted I look at this, didn't you?"

It wasn't a question, and Sarah merely smiled.

"Okay, lady. Wrap it up and leave it here. I'll submit the proposal to the planning committee first thing on Monday." Sarah began putting the papers back in her briefcase as Dan continued: "As far as I'm concerned, the deal is settled. Construction on the town will continue over the next five years, but the bulk of it will be done in two. Meanwhile, you should decide on what kind of retainer you'll want in order to hold all the stock. I don't want you selling any of my trees or roses."

"Consider them yours," Sarah said, feeling a little giddy and decidedly elated. "I think," she continued, "twenty-five percent of the total cost would be a reasonable advance. The rest, of course, won't be due until the terms of the contract are met."

"Sounds good," Dan agreed, and then extended his hand across the table for her to shake. Sarah shut her briefcase and took the offered hand, grasping it firmly in her most businesslike handshake.

"It's been delightful doing business with you," Dan said with studied politeness. "Now, will you tell me, please, if I can pursue my more personal business... with some reasonable expectation of reaching an equally satisfying conclusion? That last bit of negotiation before dinner just about ruined me."

Sarah pulled her hand away from his and laced her fingers together in her lap. Her head turned almost automatically toward the window, and she knew her face was turning pink. She didn't know what to do. Yes, business for the evening was over. Dessert had long since been cleared away. Was she going to make him wait until she had a signed piece of paper that finalized the agreement? Was she even considering making him wait until all the trees were on his property and not hers? That notion was purely absurd. And yet, she simply couldn't switch gears as quickly as he seemed able to. As her gaze cast around the lovely, warm room in which they'd spent the evening, she realized sadly that, no matter how comfortable it might be, it would always be associated in her mind with business.

As though he'd been reading her thoughts, Dan said roughly, "I see. The place is tainted. Well, it serves me right for bringing you here instead of having this meeting at your office." With a sigh of self-disgust, he rose from his seat. "Come on. I'll take you home."

Sarah gave him a grateful look that was also mixed with apology. She didn't know where to go from here. She did know that for some reason it was very important to her that he make the next move—despite the mixed messages she'd given him. She needed to be sure that now that he had her trees and roses, he still wanted her.

They drove in silence up Rock Creek Parkway and north out of the District toward Sarah's house. And when the Mercedes pulled to a halt alongside of her red Volvo, they still hadn't spoken. Dan walked her up the steps and onto the porch and waited until she'd unlocked the door. With her hand on the knob, Sarah hesitated, uncertain.

"Spend the day with me Sunday," Dan said suddenly and with a gently persuasive finger running along her arm.

She looked up at him quickly, her confusion and doubt and longing hidden only slightly in the muted yellow light from the porch lamp. Dan's look, however, was not confused. His eyes, as they met hers, held tenderness and reassurance.

"Please . . ." he smiled and gave her an encouraging wink.

Tentatively, she smiled back. "No business?"

"We'll do whatever you want to do—all day," he promised. "You call the shots."

Sarah hesitated only an instant. Then, with a quick smile of relief and pleasure that he'd made the offer, she nodded. "I'll have to work for a few hours in the morning, but I could be ready by one."

Dan gave her a shocked look. "You work on Sundays?"

Her reply was only slightly defensive. "Just to keep the irrigation system running."

He sighed. "And I thought *I* was overworked." His finger, which was still slowly stroking her arm, reached up and caressed her cheek. His eyes searched hers.

Sarah held her breath, certain he was going to kiss her again, already feeling the surge of excitement that his nearness brought.

But he didn't kiss her. Instead, he dropped his hand and, turning toward the porch steps, mumbled, "I've got to get out of here before..."

Sarah watched in stark disappointment as he hurried down the steps and toward his car, his dark form fading quickly into the shadowed darkness. "See you Sunday," she heard him call.

"Good night," she called weakly.

And then the night was filled with the quiet rumble of the car engine and the sound of crunching gravel as the headlights blazed out across the lawn. Sarah stood very still and watched until the lights had disappeared. And she wondered at the feeling of emptiness his leave-taking had brought.

- 4 -

WHEN DAN ARRIVED on Sunday, Sarah was waiting for him on the porch swing. No one looking at her would ever have thought she'd been up since dawn and had spent a good two hours kneeling in mud, sweating over a rusted pipe fitting. Her strapless sundress was snow white, with tiny pink rosebuds scattered here and there. There was a ruffle on the hem and one across the elastic top. The elastic waist made the soft cotton blouse prettily. Her hair was pulled back from her face in two golden waves, and her slender arms were stretched across the back of the swing as she rocked gently. The white sandals she wore were comfortable for walking—a deliberate choice on her part—and emphasized her slender ankles and long, smooth legs. Indeed, she was a picture of calm composure and didn't look as though she'd done anything more strenuous that day than paint her nails.

In actuality, however, her stomach churned, her heart pounded rapidly, and the palms of her hands were damp.

What she was doing was insane. Allowing herself to become involved socially with someone with whom she was doing business was breaking a cardinal rule. But for Dan Lowell, she was about ready to break all the rules. The very thought of him made her giddy with excitement.

Sarah was not so naive that she didn't recognize a large part of her excitement was pure sexual attraction. But it was more than that. His buoyant, enthusiastic approach to life, his impulsive manner, the way he went after what he wanted—all of it was new to Sarah. All of it was exciting. She felt at once threatened and irresistibly drawn. It was as if he threatened her attitudes, her security, her very way of life. And yet, with his glorious smile and mesmerizing gaze, he seemed to be offering her something much better.

None of these ambivalent feelings showed, however. Sarah had spent all of Saturday fighting a battle inside herself and had concluded that she was going to take the risk. At least for the day, she was going to enjoy herself. Terrified or not, she'd made the choice, and she wasn't sorry.

The smile she flashed Dan as he ascended the porch steps was not the least bit uncertain.

"Well, hello," he drawled lazily, leaning against a white porch column.

"Hi," she said softly. For a moment, their eyes held in a greeting that was warm and laced with pleasant anticipation. Sarah broke the contact, reaching for her small white leather shoulder bag. "Shall we go?" she asked, rising from the swing.

"Where are you taking me?" Dan inquired.

Sarah smiled slyly. "To my favorite spot in D.C.— a place everyone who lives here should go at least once, especially in the spring."

"And you aren't going to tell me what it is," he concluded with an amused chuckle.

"Trust me," she assured him. "You'll love it."

Some time later, when Sarah gave Dan directions for the final leg of the journey, she heard his breath catch and saw a look of complete bewilderment cross his features. Then, with delighted surprise, he laughed.

"The *zoo?*"

"Absolutely." Sarah smiled.

It was, of course, a wonderful idea. The weather was perfect, if a trifle warm, but they didn't notice the heat as they walked the paths of the National Zoological Park under the boughs of the huge oaks and the tall, stately tulip poplars. They ate ice cream as they circled the huge area where the big cats lived, standing for a long time in the sun to watch the rare white tiger from India. Then they strolled the relatively short distance to the monkey house, where Sarah was enchanted by the endangered and fragile-looking golden lion tamarins. They both laughed at the sight of the apes watching soap operas on the televisions in their cages. Their luck was good at the panda exhibit, where they found the two giant pandas, Ling-Ling and Hsing-Hsing, cavorting in view of a crowd of spectators; in warm weather it was unusual to get a look at the huge black and white beasts that were a gift from the People's Republic of China to the U.S.

After they left the pandas, Dan suggested they take a break.

"Sit here and wait for me," he told Sarah, guiding her to a spot on the open lawn of the park. "I'll be right back."

Sarah didn't have time to question him before he jogged off toward one of the concessions stands. When he returned, he was carrying two huge cones of pink cotton candy and wearing his most charming grin.

"I can't remember the last time I ate this stuff," he said as he plopped down cross-legged beside her.

Sarah laughed. "I remember! I was six and my father had taken me to the circus. I got very sick."

His face fell in disappointment. "I suppose I could eat both of them."

"No way," Sarah replied quickly. "Besides, as I recall, I also had four or five hot dogs and two boxes of Crackerjack that day. I deserved to get sick."

Dan's enthusiasm was restored, and he handed her one of the pink balls of spun sugar and began pulling at his own with relish.

"So, are you sorry we came to the zoo?" Sarah asked after a few minutes of sticky silence.

"*Sorry?*" Dan exclaimed. "Hell, no. I'm having a wonderful time. I just never would have guessed you'd pick a place like this."

"Shows you how much *you* know." Sarah sniffed in mock indignation.

"Obviously," he agreed, "but I'm learning . . . Give me time."

Cautiously, quietly, Sarah said, "That, I believe, is the whole point of this . . . outing."

Dan studied her for a moment, then smiled gently. "I do rush things, don't I? I'm sorry." He laughed and added, "According to my brother, Michael, it's my worst sin. He thinks it's the reason I never married . . . says I frighten women off."

Sarah looked at him thoughtfully as he applied himself to the business of licking cotton candy off his fingers. It was obvious that his words had been more than an apology; they carried a kind of warning tinged with hopefulness that he wouldn't soon find her running in the other direction.

"You know," she began slowly, "a lot of times, it seems that one's best qualities can also be one's greatest liabilities. Your way of . . . of rushing things—of taking chances, making quick decisions—has probably been a tremendous asset in making LINC such a successful company."

Dan gave her a grateful look. "It's kind of you to put it that way, and yes, I suppose you're right. But Michael, you see, isn't much interested in corporate affairs. His business is people. And he sees my, uh, shortcomings as standing in my way of *true* happiness."

"Oh?" Sarah responded curiously. "Is he a psychologist or something?"

"Or something." Dan nodded. "He's a priest—has a

huge parish in the South Bronx. He's just two years older than I, but he thinks of himself as my . . . well, my father—no pun intended."

"I understand," Sarah chuckled. "If he's in the priesthood, you must not get to see him very much. Don't a priest's duties keep him awfully busy?"

"*His* certainly do!" Dan replied. "The South Bronx is a helluva place to keep life and limb together, much less teach anything about God. He's been there a good while now and manages pretty well, all things considered . . . works himself to the bone, although he'd never admit it. Actually, I get to see him a fair amount. He coaches a couple of sports teams—baseball in the summer and wrestling in the winter. I help him out sometimes. And we work out together at the neighborhood gym every Saturday morning."

"But now you're going to be living in D.C. and won't see him at all," Sarah concluded.

Dan nodded remorsefully. "That's true. He's probably the only reason I regret leaving New York. I'll still be going back and forth every so often, of course. We aren't closing down New York operations entirely." And then, as though he'd thought enough about what he'd left behind, Dan stood up, saying, "Let's walk some more. We've still got the snakes and seals and birds to see."

Sarah took his offered hand and let him pull her to her feet. She was about to walk toward the pavement when Dan's hand on her arm stopped her.

"Just a minute," he said with a curious frown. "Gotta check for pink sugar first."

Sarah looked down quickly at her dress and then at her sticky hands, one of which still held the half-eaten fluff. "Have I got it all over me?" she asked.

"Just one spot," he replied. "Right . . . here." And he leaned down to kiss her quickly before she realized his intentions.

It was a sticky kiss and a sweet one. Nothing touched except their lips, but Sarah felt as though she were bound, hand and foot. And given the fact that they were very

much in public, it was probably even an acceptable sort
of kiss for appearances' sake; but Sarah felt her insides
turning to liquid and thought she might just melt like her
cotton candy as Dan's firm and persuasive mouth coaxed
hers into a clinging response.

"Hmm," he said, pulling away just a fraction and
running his tongue over her bottom lip once more. "Delicious."

Sarah turned her head and blushed.

Dan sighed. "Don't tell me: Too fast again, right?"

Sarah glanced at him quickly and then away again.
"N-no," she managed, "not too fast. It...you startled
me. And, well, we're in public."

"Phew!" Dan breathed in relief. "Well, if that's all it
is, then we're making progress!" He hooked one strong
arm around her waist and pulled her against his side.
"Come on. Let's go get a look at the snakes."

And so they ate their cotton candy and walked the
rest of the way to the far entrance of the zoo, stopping
at the exhibits along the way. When they reached the
visitor's center, they made use of the rest rooms to wash
their very sticky fingers and met once more at the Connecticut Avenue gate to begin the long trek back down
to the parking lot.

"These are some hills you've got to climb around
here," Dan commented as they started along the path to
the birdhouse.

"We've just climbed out of Rock Creek Park," Sarah
replied. She was about to comment further on the park
itself, but Dan stopped short. She looked up at him and
was puzzled by the frown she saw. Glancing quickly at
the walk in front of them, she asked, "Is something
wrong?"

"I'm willing to bet there is," he replied. And then he
was guiding her to the right.

Sarah was surprised but immediately understood when
they stopped in front of a small, dark-haired girl who
looked to be about five years old and was obviously of
Hispanic background. The child was standing—fro-

zen—beside a bench and large trash can, the look in her huge doelike brown eyes unmistakable in any language. She was terrified.

Dan hunkered down in front of the girl, who turned those enormous eyes on him. "Hi," he said with a smile. "Are you waiting for your mom or dad?" The girl stared at him in bewilderment and then turned imploring eyes up to Sarah.

"The poor kid, I'll bet she's lost," Sarah said soothingly, and squatted down alongside Dan.

"Where's your mom, sweetheart?" Dan queried gently. "Can't you find her?"

When the girl remained silent, Sarah sighed. "You wouldn't just happen to speak Spanish, would you?" Sarah hadn't meant it seriously, and at Dan's next words, her eyes widened in surprise.

"Donde estás tu madre, niña?"

That got results. Without further comment, the little girl burst into tears, and with them came a long stream of what sounded, to Sarah's ears, like babble. Dan, however, didn't seem the least bit deterred. He listened for a few minutes and then spoke again. After several more ragged responses from their tearful charge, he looked over at Sarah.

"Her name is Florencia Alvarez and she's six. She's been waiting here for the longest time, she says. The last time she saw her mother was inside the visitor's center. She got interested in a picture and didn't notice when the family left the building."

Then turning back to Florencia, Dan grinned reassuringly and spoke once more. The girl seemed to hesitate for a second before flinging herself into his open and inviting arms.

"Now!" Dan said as he straightened with Florencia clinging to his neck, "let's find ourselves a park policeman or security guard or something."

"There should be someone in the office at the visitor's center," Sarah suggested, and Dan nodded as they headed back toward the building up the hill.

Indeed, there was someone to help at the visitor's center—someone in the form of a very upset Mrs. Alvarez, who'd been looking for her daughter for over an hour. Her cry of relief at the sight of Florencia being carried in Dan's arms into the center's office made Sarah feel like crying herself. She smiled warmly at the sight of Dan handing the child over to her sobbing mother.

It was a joyful reunion. Mrs. Alvarez thanked Dan and Sarah profusely in a mixture of English and Spanish. How reassuring it was upon leaving her home in Argentina to find such good people in *los Estados Unidos*. It seemed her husband was a lower-echelon employee at the Argentinian embassy and they'd only been in the country a month. They were just beginning to take their children to see the sights.

When the world had been restored to normal, Sarah and Dan started off again toward the birdhouse.

"You handled that pretty well," Sarah commented as they walked.

Dan shrugged. "I like children. It was obvious she was in trouble."

"Don't be so modest," Sarah chided gently. "You were great. She trusted you instantly." As Dan continued to walk with his hands in his pockets, looking down at the ground, Sarah couldn't help laughing. "Hey, come on! Don't tell me you're embarrassed? Admit it. You said and did all the right things, and that little girl fell in love with you on sight."

A slow grin spread on Dan's face. "If I speak Spanish and carry you home, will you fall in love with me, too?" He glanced at her sideways with a twinkle of amusement in his blue eyes.

But Sarah wasn't sure he was kidding. Her eyes narrowed suspiciously. "You'd better not try carrying me even as far as the aviary!" she replied, keeping the tone of her reply light. "I'll kick and scream the entire way."

"Is that a promise?" he asked, raising one brow in challenge.

Sarah started to back away. "Uh-oh, no you don't . . ."

she began, and when he started after her, she took off, laughing.

He chased her all the way to the aviary, where they breathlessly climbed to the top of the high net-covered tower and then stood gasping. That is, Sarah stood gasping. Dan was hardly winded. They stayed there for a long time watching feathered creatures of all sizes and colors fly around and over and under them. It was an enchanted world and one of Sarah's favorite places at the zoo.

By the time they left the birds, the sun was starting to sink and turn everything a mellow, burnt gold.

"I'm almost afraid to ask what you had in mind for dinner," Dan said as they walked toward the car.

"You can't be hungry after all the junk you've eaten," Sarah scoffed with an incredulous look.

Dan looked back at her, held her gaze for a moment, and replied, "I'm starving."

It was abundantly clear that he wasn't thinking about food.

"Steaks," Sarah stated flatly. "I've got two home in the fridge, waiting for the grill. I thought you might appreciate a meal that you didn't have to order from a menu for a change."

Dan's expression changed from one of lightly veiled lust to pleased surprise. "Can we roast marshmallows?" he asked.

Sarah laughed. "You've got to be kidding!" When his face fell slightly and it was clear that he was not, she laughed harder. "All right, all right. But we'll have to stop and get them. Marshmallows aren't on my regular grocery list."

While they were waiting for the fire to die down in the charcoal grill and the wine to chill in the refrigerator, Sarah and Dan worked together in the kitchen on the other meal preparations. Dan refused to sit and watch Sarah cook; rather, he plunged into making a dressing for the salad that he said was an old family secret. Sarah was dubious at first, but soon relaxed when it became apparent that Dan was more than familiar with the workings of a kitchen. Still, as she sliced avocado and green pepper and watched him rummaging through her spice cabinet, it was a bit unnerving to see just what he put into the blender. But she bit her tongue and hoped for the best.

Later she was glad she had. The dressing was delicious. The steaks were perfect. The rice pilaf she'd thrown together was just right. And all together, it was a delightful meal.

The conversation was pleasant, too. With some encouragement, Dan regaled her with anecdotes about growing up in New York and stories about the sports teams he had helped his brother to coach. He was witty, observant, and charming, but he never gave Sarah the feeling that he was trying to impress her or even that he particularly wanted to talk about himself. She had to ask the questions, and although Dan answered them readily enough, she was sure he would not have offered all the personal information if she hadn't asked. No one would ever accuse Dan Lowell of being humble, but he wasn't a show-off either. And Sarah liked him all the more for it.

In fact, she liked him very much. The entire day in his company had been a pleasure. There'd been the constant undercurrent of sexual attraction between them that had flared up now and then, but it had never gotten in the way of their simple enjoyment in being together. It had been just the sort of day she'd needed. She felt so comfortable . . .

"Now it's time for dessert!"

"What?" Sarah responded distractedly.

"You're a million miles away," Dan accused gently as he smiled at her from across the table. They'd decided to eat their meal in the less formal atmosphere of the country kitchen rather than use the large dining room. "What are you thinking?" he asked.

Sarah smiled a little secretively. "Oh, just thinking how nice the day has been. I haven't taken a day off just to play in a long time."

Dan wagged a finger at her. "You should play more often, Sarah Turner. I've never seen you look this relaxed before. Play seems to agree with you."

And so do you agree with me, Sarah could have added. Instead, she said, "Well, maybe after I replace my old irrigation system, I'll have more—" Her words were choked off as she remembered the very thing play had forced from her mind. "Oh, Dan! I completely forgot. I've got to go make sure the water has turned itself off. If I don't, the rose fields may be drowned! I should have checked when I got home!" She pushed her chair away from the table and hurriedly stacked her plates in the sink.

Dan's jaw dropped. "You must be joking. You really can't be thinking of traipsing out in the dark to check on the roses!"

"I wish I *were* joking," she mumbled sadly. "But I'm not. It'll only take a few minutes, really. I'll just jump in the car and run over to section three. I'll be back here before you've had a chance to eat two marshmallows. I promise."

"What if the water hasn't turned itself off?" he asked uncertainly.

She sighed remorsefully, then said with a grin, "I'll come back and call Tom. He'll come fix it for me." She held out both hands in supplication. "Look, I won't even change my clothes. That way I can't get tied up with the plumbing. You put the marshmallows on the sticks and I'll be back." She grabbed her keys off the hook at the back door and was gone before he had another chance to talk her out of it.

Sarah was actually only gone fifteen minutes. She came skipping breathlessly through the back door, saying, "See? I told you...Dan! Oh, you shouldn't have done it!" At the sight of the clean dishes draining and the spotless counters, she turned to him with a dismayed look. "That's a rotten way to treat a guest. My reputation as a hostess will be ruined forever!"

Dan dried the last pot, which had been used to make the rice pilaf, and hung the dish towel on the rack on the cabinet door under the sink. "Don't be ridiculous," he said. "If you have to go to work on a Sunday night, the least I can do is wash a couple of dishes. Besides, believe it or not, I actually like doing it."

"Come on," Sarah said disbelievingly. "Nobody likes doing dishes."

He shrugged. "I do."

She eyed him suspiciously. "You know, for a rich land baron—Wall Street tycoon, you're awfully domestic."

He turned to her and grinned. "A man doesn't get to be a thirty-nine-year-old bachelor who's always lived alone without learning to do a few things for himself."

"Some men do," she countered.

"Some men don't know how to enjoy life either," he replied. "I happen to enjoy making salad dressing and washing dishes."

"Do you do windows?" she asked hopefully.

"Not a chance," was his quick reply. And at her look of mock disappointment, he added, "But I do scrub a mean floor, and I'm quite expert at ironing, although I haven't had much practice on, uh, feminine apparel."

"How are you at roasting marshmallows?"

"Ah!" Dan walked toward her, picking up the plastic bag lying on the table. "Now, that's a real art. Come on, I'll show you."

Twenty minutes later, having searched for and found the ultimate in marshmallow-roasting sticks, Sarah was sitting back on the lounge chair in her backyard, licking marshmallow off her fingers, while Dan toasted her third round over the glowing embers.

"Hmm," she sighed. "You're right. It's an art . . . and I think you've got it."

"I take it you're ready for another one," he said, turning toward her with the stick in his hand. On its end two plump, perfectly golden marshmallows were impaled.

"I could eat the whole bag," she answered cheerfully, "but I'll settle for one more."

She drew up her feet as Dan sat sideways on the bottom end of the lounge and twisted to face her. Carefully he pulled off the marshmallow on the end and handed it to her.

"It's hot," he warned her. As he said it his fingers brushed hers, sending little tingles of awareness up Sarah's arm.

Her hand shook as she handled the molten sugar. To cover her unexpected surge of nervousness over his touch, she said, "I've watched you consume ice cream, cotton candy, countless soft drinks, and now marshmallows—all in one day. I'd say you have a serious sweet tooth."

Dan, who had been picking at his own marshmallow, looked up and smiled wickedly. "Compensation," he said softly. "What I'd really like to have isn't on the menu."

Sarah stopped cold with her index finger in her mouth, as she was licking off the last of the white goo. The outdoor lanterns she'd lit and the yellow porch light cast shadows across the lawn and bathed the two of them in the glow. There wasn't any doubt in Sarah's mind about what she was reading in Dan's firelit gaze. Her heart pounded and she suddenly felt a shiver go up her spine.

"Cold?" Dan asked quietly.

She hesitated for just a second and then, too quickly, shook her head. "No, but I was just thinking of fixing some coffee." She swung her legs off the opposite side of the lounge and rose. "Do you want to come inside?" she asked shakily. "Or I could bring it out."

Dan looked up at her over his shoulder for an instant. Then, with deliberate movements, he finished the last of his marshmallow, broke the stick into several pieces, and got up to walk over to the grill. He fed the used stick to the dying embers and said, "I'll come in."

Sarah didn't wait for him but hurried toward the house. *Why now?* she thought. Why, after having a perfectly marvelous day—one almost completely free of emotional tension—was she suddenly turning into a basket case? But the answer was obvious. The day was over. Or rather, it should be over. It had been wonderful, but it was time to say a polite good night and send Dan on his way.

And if it hadn't been for one simple fact, that would have been a relatively easy thing to do, the simple fact being that they both wanted the day to end differently. The problem was that Sarah wasn't sure she was ready for it to end any other way. Once more she was caught in the welter of complex and ambivalent feelings.

Sarah hated making decisions. It wasn't that she wasn't good at making them. And once they were made, she stuck by them and saw them through. But the moment she had to commit herself, to take that leap into the great beyond, along with the risk that there might be nothing under her . . . well, that was something she avoided whenever possible. She always did the safe thing, the expected thing.

And where had it ever gotten her?

The screen door banged as Dan came into the kitchen. Sarah jumped and spilled some coffee out of the measuring spoon and onto the counter.

"Sit down," she said brightly, her voice sounding brittle to her own ears. "The coffee maker only takes a few minutes."

Dan didn't reply, although she heard the scrape of a chair behind her as she poured water through the top of the applicance. She knew he was watching her every move, and it made her nervous—so nervous that she knocked the sugar bowl over, spilling the white granules down into the sink and all over the floor.

Sarah reached quickly for a sponge. Dan was beside her instantly, taking it from her shaking fingers and tossing it into the sink as the other hand cupped her chin and made her look at him.

"Sarah, I don't want a cup of coffee," he said quietly, in a voice that made Sarah think of brandy and cream. "What I want," he continued, "is to put my mouth on yours. I want to take this dress off you and look at you— all of you—with the light on. I want to touch and taste your lips and shoulders and breasts and . . ."

Sarah groaned softly as Dan continued the delineation of the journey he would take across her body in terms so explicit, so shocking, so completely erotic, that she felt her skin tingle, her nipples tauten, and her womb grow heavy with throbbing, aching desire. When he'd completed his verbal passage, the only place he'd touched her was where his hand still cupped her face; yet, Sarah knew she was thoroughly and hopelessly seduced.

"Now, Sarah," Dan said with maddening persistence, "tell me: Do you really want a cup of coffee?"

The thought was blasphemous. Her answer was immediately apparent in her eyes and hardly needed the tiny shake of her head and the whispered "No."

He waited, and when she didn't continue of her own accord, he pressed the issue home. "And what do you want?" he asked, knowing full well the answer and insisting that she say it.

Her heart pounding, unable to look at him any longer, Sarah buried her face against his chest.

"You," she said softly. "I want you."

"Thank God," he muttered thickly, his mouth muffled in her hair. And then he bent and lifted her into his arms, and she clung to his neck. "You tell me if I make a wrong turn," he said, walking purposefully out of the kitchen.

But he didn't make any wrong turns. He carried her down the long hallway and up the wide, bare wood stairs, which creaked just as they always had for as long as Sarah could remember. He turned unerringly into her room, walking straight to the bed to stand her carefully beside it. Then he reached behind her to switch on the bedside lamp.

"How did you know this one was mine?" she asked.

"Instinct," he replied, pulling her to him. His hands cupping her face, his mouth brushed hers lightly—once. And then, with a racking shudder, Dan's arms enveloped her and his mouth came down in a kiss that left Sarah breathless.

Nothing in her experience had prepared her for this kiss. All the restraints were gone. He wasn't going to

stop this time. His mouth and his hands and his eyes told
her as nothing else could that the deal was made. There
would be no reneging on this contract. He'd explained
the terms, and his lips moving confidently against hers,
his tongue finding and tasting all the hidden recesses of
her mouth, and his breath warm and ragged, mingling
with her own, all said that he intended to carry out those
terms to the last detail.

His fingers hooked the elastic top of her dress and he
slowly eased the fabric down to her waist. With his hands
resting gently on her arms, he paused in the execution
of his plan long enough to look at what he'd uncovered.
His eyes blazed and his breath caught as he reached out
to touch the porcelain-white skin. One finger of each
hand moved slowly, deftly, around the dusky center of
each breast. And he watched, fascinated, as the nipples
hardened into throbbing buds.

"You're so beautiful," he murmured, touching each
breast almost reverently.

Sarah moaned, not knowing whether the pleasure came
from what he was doing to her now or the anticipation
of what she knew he was planning to do to her next.
When he bent and kissed that which he had so aroused,
she could hardly stand the shooting currents of intense
pleasure stabbing through her. She reached almost desperately for the front of Dan's shirt, tugging as though
the buttons would open magically. When she realized
they wouldn't, a frustrated sound escaped her, and she
made her fingers work. Dan straighted to allow her easier
access, and she glanced up to meet his intense gaze, his
eyes now darkened to a liquid sapphire. His look told
her she'd get no help undressing him. Those were the
unspoken terms of the contract. He wanted to know that
she wanted him as much as he wanted her. And, God
help her, she did!

Never had she wanted anyone the way she wanted
him! It was shameless, wanton. She gave up the struggle
to analyze her impulses, to try to make them less overwhelming and more manageable, and simply let them
take her. This was passion, and she'd never really felt

it before. There was something else, too . . . something
that had to do with longing and tenderness and a sense
of rightness; but she couldn't make herself think about
that yet. And it didn't matter. Nothing mattered except
satisfying the driving need to know the man who stood
breathing heavily and trembling under her not-too-steady
hands.

Finally, Sarah tugged Dan's shirt free of his slacks
and undid the last button. Then it was heaven to lay her
hands flat against the hard-muscled wall of his chest, to
see her fingers splayed over the different textures and
contours of his skin and the thick mat of dark hair that
swirled around the puckered male nipples and ran in a
silky line down his flat abdomen to disappear below his
belt. She'd known his body would be beautiful, but the
sight and feel of it took her breath away.

Sarah had hardly begun to satisfy her need to touch
him when Dan took her hands and held them at her sides.
Slowly, as they both watched, he leaned forward, and
Sarah felt that dark hair tickling the skin on her breasts,
her stomach, her chest.

"Touch me this way, Sarah," Dan said huskily. "Touch
me."

Obediently, Sarah melted against him and groaned as
heated flesh met heated flesh. Her gaze rose to his and
then their arms were around each other, drawing them
closer and closer as their mouths drank once more of that
endless well of passion they'd discovered.

Dan tugged the elastic of her dress over the swell of
her hips, letting his touch linger on each exposed curve.
Then he was stooping to pull off her garments—her dress
and half-slip and lacy underwear. She couldn't remember
what had happened to her shoes.

Dan's eyes traveled slowly up along her body. His
hands followed, learning the contours of her slender legs,
the silken feel of her thighs. His arm came around her
hips and he pulled her to him, burying his face against
the soft skin of her belly. His lips moved across her flesh
as his hand moved up her inner thigh, parting her legs,
moving up higher, until . . .

"Dan!" Sarah gasped. "Please, I—I can't stand up anymore."

He mumbled something incoherent, and her hands gripped his shoulders when, rather than heeding her plea, his mouth moved to replace his fingers. Sarah cried out in pleasure and in agony—unable to make him stop, unable to keep her knees from giving way beneath her. When she thought she would surely fall, Dan's hand snaked around her and snatched the counterpane off the bed in one billowing sweep. His hands gripped the soft curve of her buttocks and urged her backward until she had no choice but to fall.

And he followed, never lessening the sweet torture that he wrought upon her most vulnerable places. It was wicked. It was indescribably wonderful. Sarah's head was reeling. Her fingers fluttered through the dark silk of his hair until instinct made her tug—at first weakly and then with some urgency—urging him to come up to her.

Reluctantly and with a soft chuckle, he complied, laying his still half-clothed body down along the length of hers. "You've still got some work to do, lady." He grinned. "I hope you're as impatient as I am."

Instantly, Sarah's fingers were at his belt, and then she was shoving his slacks and shorts together down over his lean hips. She was too far gone to be embarrassed or to take much time about it. She had to kneel to remove his clothes completely, and she smiled to herself when she saw that *he*'d lost his shoes, too. The dark socks were dispensed with quickly, and then she turned—half sitting on her heels—to look unabashedly at him lying on his back, one arm behind his head, one lying across her side of the bed.

Their eyes met: his gaze possessive and bold and very, very blue; hers soft and passion-drugged and a deep emerald green.

Sarah's eyes took in the masculine form she'd laid bare. Dan watched her perusal. And he didn't move as her fingers followed her eyes, although Sarah could hear his breathing grow faster and more ragged. She traced the hard line of muscle in his thigh and the line of hair down his stomach, which had previously stopped at his belt. Then she let her fingers find their way to the taut flesh of his boldly aroused masculinity. She lingered there, fascinated, as he had been when he'd discovered her breasts. And Sarah marveled at the pulsing, throbbing contractions she felt between her legs, her body's instinctive reaction to what her hand touched.

With a low, feral growl, Dan reached for her, and Sarah found herself on her back, her hair a tumbled curtain of gold across her face and over the pillow. Dan smoothed the hair off her face tenderly as he lowered his body onto hers. His thighs spread her own until hers were resting atop those hard, flexing muscles she'd so recently touched. His hands cupped her face as he leaned over her and their eyes locked.

"Sarah..." he breathed, as slowly, inexorably, his body entered hers. Sarah sobbed at the unspeakable joy of having him inside of her, filling her, taking that part of her that so longed to be taken.

"Oh, God, Sarah!" Dan cried hoarsely. "You feel so good...so good!" His arm slipped under her hips to raise her to him as she gasped his name.

"Dan!...Oh, yes, like that..."

Sarah felt her bones melting at the exquisite intimacy, the undeniable knowledge that his flesh was buried deep, deep inside of hers. There was only one thing that could bind them further, and inevitably Dan began the movement that would take them that last step.

Sarah's eyes closed; Dan's arm under her tightened. His hips moved and hers met his. And she kept meeting him, her body totally involved in this act, which required complete agreement, undoubting trust, total honesty. There was no mercy given. When the tension in her body had built to a blinding, unequaled heat, Sarah found herself clinging to Dan, her fingers digging into his back and the hard flesh of his buttocks. Her head moved back and forth on the pillow, and she gasped back tiny little moans that begged for release. Dan's mouth captured hers and held her still as he gasped, "Oh, Sarah, Yes. Now!"

"Now, Sarah!"

The long, throaty groan started deep inside of her and went on and on as her body arched under him. Her eyes flew open and green melted into blue as the shuddering, convulsive wave rocked them both in pulsing, rhythmically perfect moments of endless blending, timeless pleasure, and soul-shattering ecstasy.

Long, long minutes later, Sarah's hand ran languorously up the sweet-slick flesh of Dan's back. His head moved slightly on the pillow beside her, and his lips tasted of the salty drops on her cheek. A final tremor ran through her and she sighed. Eventually, their heartbeats slowed and their breathing became normal again. When he tried to leave her, she whimpered and clutched him tighter.

He smiled down at her tenderly and pushed a wet lock of gold silk off her brow. "Will you let me turn out the light?" he asked softly.

Her face relaxed and she nodded. He moved to her side and accomplished the task. Then he reached down to pull the sheet up as far as their waists before lying down again and pulling her to him.

"It's ungodly hot in here, but I want you next to me," he said quietly.

"Oh!" Sarah cried softly and pushed away from him. Before he could protest she was off the bed and opening the window. Turning on the big window fan, she said, "I always close it in case of a storm."

He chuckled. "The problem is, the only storm around here tonight needed all the air it could get . . . Come back here."

She climbed back onto the bed and nestled beside him, enjoying the cooler breeze now wafting over their hot bodies. Sarah reached up to trace his lips with her finger. He caught the tip between his teeth and bit gently.

"Sarah?" he whispered.

"Hmmm?"

"Spend some time with me this week, Sarah." There was a boyish note in his plea.

Sarah's voice held only a fraction of her disappointment. "I can't. With the weather being so unseasonably hot, I have to stay on the irrigation systems."

"But I'm on vacation in a lonely city. What fun is vacationing alone?"

"Dan," she sighed, "I'd love to keep you company this week, but I just can't take off work."

"Can I tag along with you, then?"

There was a brief moment of silence before Sarah stated flatly, "You're kidding. Right?"

"No, I'm not," he replied. "If you refuse, I'll probably do it anyway, so you might as well say yes. Besides, if they're *my* plants you're going to be watering, I should get to know them."

"You really do want them all, don't you," she said gently, still amazed at the notion and the turn her life had taken.

"I'd have settled for the roses," he answered sleepily.

"Well, haven't the others . . . grown on you?"

"Please!" Dan exclaimed with a soft, mellow laugh. "Go to sleep. I haven't slept since I laid eyes on you last Tuesday, and making love in a sauna has worn me out. On top of that, I've got a week in the blazing sun to look forward to. I'm not up to exchanging puns right now."

"Yes, sir." Sarah giggled and snuggled back against him as though she'd been doing it for years.

"I hope you've got another one of those ridiculous sun hats," Dan grumbled as his arm moved to encircle her waist. "I work hard to keep my unhealthy office pallor."

"How about a ski mask?" Sarah suggested.

"How about you stop wriggling so I can go to sleep?"

But she didn't, and so he couldn't. And soon they found sleep the farthest thing from their minds. It was very late when they finally fell asleep, wrapped in each other's arms, listening to the sound of thunder rolling outside the open window.

- 5 -

THE CRICKETLIKE ELECTRONIC chirping of the phone beside the bed finally awakened Sarah. She blinked, disconcerted to find herself on the wrong side of the bed, and tried to roll over to answer it. But she couldn't move. Her legs were pinned under a lead weight, and there was a wall of unyielding rock behind her. Then her mind cleared and she remembered just what the wall was. The ringing of the telephone persisted, however, and so she extricated herself from Dan's possessive hold to stretch— none too gracefully—across his sleeping form for the receiver. As she did, her eyes focused on the alarm clock and widened in shock.

"Hullo," she croaked in a sleep-drugged voice.

"Sarah?" Betty's voice sounded concerned. "Are you all right?"

"Fine," Sarah mumbled. "Just forgot to set the clock. I'm sorr*iiieee*!"

An arm slipped around her waist, and suddenly she

80

found herself sprawled on top of Dan's not-so-sleepy body.

"Sarah?" Betty exclaimed. "What happened? Are you okay?"

"I'm fine!" Sarah snapped, and then with her hand over the receiver she hissed, "Stop it! You're worrying Betty half to death!"

"You think she's worried now?" Dan chuckled. "Just you wait'll she finds out what you did last night."

Sarah rolled her eyes and spoke once more into the receiver. "I'll be a while longer, Betts—at least another hour. Okay?"

"Sarah, are you sick?" Betty was clearly not convinced that Sarah was telling her the whole story.

"No!" Sarah cried, realizing that if Betty really thought she was ill, she'd be over in five minutes to take her temperature. "I'm fine! I'm just late, that's all."

"Uh-huh," Betty replied tentatively. "Tom and I were just wondering where you were. You're never late."

Sarah sighed. "Well, then it's about time, isn't it? I'll see you later."

She barely had time to return the phone to its cradle before she found herself on her back with Dan sprawled across her.

"Good morning, beautiful," he said in a low, dreamy sort of way.

"I'm never beautiful in the morning," she countered.

"Sarah, you'd be beautiful in a potato sack with mud plastered all over your face."

"That's absurd," she chided, but couldn't suppress a tiny smile.

"That's not absurd," he argued with a shake of his dark, tousled head. "Later I might tell you what it is, but for now..." His lips descended to nibble at hers, and Sarah let her arms wind around his neck to pull him closer.

His last comment had confused her, and she would have pressed him to explain about mud and what was and wasn't absurd, but then his mouth made its way

downward across her throat and chest and began teasing
one pink nipple into arousal. She sighed and gave herself
up to this early-morning peace and pleasure as the sun
poured in through the lace curtains. In the oak outside
the open window, a cardinal began its morning song.
Sarah's fingers wandered across the silky darkness of
Dan's hair, delighting in the texture and thickness. For
at least a full minute, nothing disturbed the delicious air
of contentment that had settled over the quiet room.

And then Sarah remembered what she had to do that
day. With a frown, she asked, "Are we going to make
love before breakfast?"

Dan laughed softly against the white globe of her
breast. "Ah, mavourneen, I'm a-thinkin' we'll be makin'
love from now till the sun sets."

Sarah's eyes widened in amusement and surprise at
the lilt of his Irish brogue. "What does that word mean?"
she asked. "Mav . . ."

"Mavourneen," he whispered huskily. "A lovely word
it is, too, me darlin' Sarah. It means just that—me darlin'."

Sarah trembled with pleasure—whether at the sound
of his voice, his words, or his lips on her flesh, she didn't
know. All of them, she supposed. Every part of him was
rich and softly mellow and full. Dan's lips burned a slow,
lazy trail up to her neck, and in its wake her skin tingled.
She was loath to stop him, but it was late, and she had
to think about work . . . She sighed with remorse at the
thought.

"Dan . . . If we keep this up, who's going to water
your roses?"

"I knew ye'd be seein' the problem that way," he
crooned, all the while nibbling gently at her earlobe.
"It's me plan to keep ye abed till ye agree to take some
wee bit o' time to play with me this week."

"You'd do it, too, wouldn't you?" she murmured. Her
head was already starting to reel in what was becoming
a familiar way; he simply wouldn't take no for an answer,
and he employed the most devastating methods of achiev-

ing his goals. She felt dizzy trying to keep up with him, but just then it was a very pleasant way to feel.

"Ah, now ye're beginnin' to learn the way o' things," he said gently as his fingers applied delicate pressure to the rosy-colored nipple trapped between them. "If'n ye be concerned for the well-bein' of me precious roses, ye'll say yes to me now an' we can be gettin' on with the day. But if'n ye be stubborn, ye might find ye're no good for work *or* play. For I'll see to it that ye're too tired to walk by mornin'."

Sarah gave a tiny gasp as his fingers continued their tender seduction, moving lower to spread her thighs for his assault. "Maybe a *little* tired wouldn't be bad," she said breathlessly, and then found herself crying his name in pleasure at the speed with which he began to make good his word.

Two hours later, at eleven o'clock, Sarah walked into the nursery office with Dan following behind her. She'd given in to the inevitable and agreed to take time off to see him, knowing she couldn't really afford it but knowing he would keep pressing until she agreed. And the prospects of spending time with him and enjoying the sights of D.C., going out to dinner—making love— were really too tempting to resist. And why should she resist them?

As Sarah and Dan entered the nursery office, Betty looked up from her typewriter and her eyes widened above her reading glasses.

"Good morning, Betts!" Sarah said breezily. "Mail here yet?"

Betty stammered unintelligibly as she continued to stare at Dan, who stood smiling at her crookedly as he lounged against Sarah's office door.

"Good morning, Betty," he said. "It's going to be another hot day, isn't it? Quite unusual, I understand, for this time of year in Maryland."

Betty scowled warily. "'Mornin', Mr. Lowell. I guess the weather is about what it usually is around here. Un-

predictable ... like some people I know." Her gaze shifted
to Sarah, who was bent over the desk, rooting through
the mail. "Your mail is on your desk," she said. "Mrs.
Larson called wanting to know if you have any more of
those apricot deciduous azaleas. And a Mr. Thorpe called
from Connecticut looking for some unpronounceable thing
that somebody told him we've got. I wrote it down and
laid it on your desk, but it doesn't look like anything
I've seen on any inventory sheet. Besides that"—she
gave Sarah a disgusted look—"the water's out again.
Tom's working on it now." Then Betty glanced briefly
at Dan before asking, "Are you going to be available
today?"

"Of course I'm available," Sarah said as she straightened. "Whatever makes you think I'm not?" And only
the completely innocent look she directed at the older
woman kept Betty from further comment.

Dan cleared his throat and stepped inside Sarah's office.

"Betty, where's that box containing my father's nursery uniforms? Dan is going to sort of follow me around
today, and he'll need something to wear."

Her mouth set in a straight line, Betty answered with
obvious reluctance, "I'll get them," and rose from her
desk to comply.

"Thanks!" Sarah shot over her shoulder as she went
into her office, closing the door behind her. "Lord! There
are times ..." she began threateningly.

"She'd never take you seriously if you fired her," Dan
chuckled from where he had sprawled on the worn leather
couch.

Sarah grimaced. "You're right. She'd come to work
anyway and write her own paycheck every Friday, just
like always. Besides, she's like my mother. You can't
fire your mother. Ever since Jane Turner moved to Oregon, she's ... Well, that's a long story." Sarah waved
her hand in dismissal as she sank into the chair behind
her desk.

"She'll get used to me," he assured her.

Sarah cocked a brow. "Don't hold your breath." And

then, turning her attention to more pressing issues, she said, "I have to decide what to do with clients who want to buy nursery stock. I can't sell things I don't own."

"I'm not attached to the apricot azaleas." Dan grinned. "If the lady is really anxious, go ahead. And if you have any prior orders, of course, you have to fill them. Essentially, however, you're right. I want you to consider the deal closed."

Sarah nodded in confirmation.

"In fact," Dan continued thoughtfully, "the best thing would be for me to have a bank draft for you this afternoon. I'll call them and take a ride down there. Then there won't be any question."

Sarah started to agree again and then stopped. She hesitated. Yes, it made sense; but somehow she hadn't imagined it was all going to be settled so quickly. Not that she wasn't overjoyed about selling the stock; however, the idea of getting rid of all of it—and some of it she'd grown up seeing practically every day—took a little getting used to. And, too, she'd hoped she would be discussing the money aspects of the contract with someone besides Dan. She didn't want the money to come directly from him; she wanted to be able to deal with this on a more professional level, even if the money actually came from Dan's company.

"Oh, Dan," she began with a careless wave of her hand, "it isn't necessary. We don't even have a signed contract yet. I can wait another week or so."

"But you shouldn't have to wait," Dan insisted. "You'll have the agreed-upon twenty-five percent today. Then you won't have to wonder what to do—and the business part of our relationship will be over."

So he wanted it over with, too—or was he just being considerate of her nervous quirks? "What if you're planning committee revolts?" she asked.

"They have no choice in the matter," Dan replied cheerfully.

"That's a very strange planning committee you've got," Sarah remarked dryly.

Dan laughed as he rose from the couch and walked

over to sit on the edge of her desk, facing her. "Mavourneen, don't you see?" He grinned at the blush his brogue brought to her cheeks. He'd seen to it that she would always associate the sound of it with their lovemaking. "It'll be but a little thing to charm them into me own way o' thinkin'," he continued. "They know well that in me they've found their leprechaun. I've a knack, it seems, for findin' me way to a pot o' gold at the end of every rainbow. They'd be fools, indeed, to try to stop me from gettin' there, now, would they not?"

Sarah studied his face with its crooked smile and its blue eyes twinkling with the sheer delight of living. She shook her head slowly and smiled. "You know," she said thoughtfully, "your talents are truly being wasted.

Dan raised one affronted eyebrow at her.

"I'd bet," she continued, "that if the government would let you try, by the end of the week, you'd have the Soviets agreeing to total disarmament—and by the weekend, you'd have OPEC shipping its oil to us for free."

The afternoon brought a moment's tension when Sarah announced to Betty and Tom that Dan had bought the entire stock of the Ashcroft Nursery with the exception of the contents of the greenhouses. She explained to their further astonishment that the following spring they would be gearing up to move trees and roses to their new homes as construction on the new town, Rosecroft, was completed.

"Why's he doing this?" Betty demanded to know.

"Because he likes what we've got to sell," Sarah replied evenly. She was glad Dan had gone to the bank. She'd expected Tom and Betty to be shocked—she still was herself—but she hadn't expected them to be outright hostile toward the idea.

"You sure he wants the trees?" Tom asked, his eyes narrow. "Or is it that he wanted you bad enough to buy them?"

Sarah was speechless. She looked at the man who had known her since she was in a playpen and felt herself getting red with suppressed anger. "Just what are you implying, Tom Swenson?" she asked carefully.

Tom shrugged. "I'm not blaming you, Sarah. Don't go getting yourself riled. The man's got a reputation from here to kingdom come and back again, and it's just plain sensible to consider what his motives are."

"I don't know a thing about any reputation," Sarah said tartly, wondering where Tom had gotten such information—and not really surprised that he had. "But I *do* know that whatever passes between Dan and me hasn't anything to do with the business we transact between LINC and Ashcroft. He came here in the first place to buy roses. He knew before he ever met me that he wanted them. When he saw the rest of the stock, he asked me to draw up a proposal and a map for him. I did, and he liked it, and that's that."

And that *was* that, she decided. Somehow, putting it in such definitive terms made the whole picture much clearer.

"Hmph," Betty snorted in disgust. "I've known all along you should've been getting out and meeting more men. You've been working yourself to death since Bill died. You were easy prey for the likes of that sweet-talking Irishman."

"Betty," Sarah began calmly enough, "did it occur to you that if I had wanted to get out and meet men, I would have done so?" And then her voice began to shake a bit. "I'm *not* a child! And I just don't understand why the two of you are so dead set against the man." She waved her hands in frustration. "You don't even know him!"

"And neither do you!" Betty retorted. "He's just an Irish—"

"For God's sake," Sarah exclaimed, "so are you!"

Betty gave her a look as though to say that fact alone should convince Sarah that she knew more about Dan than Sarah did.

"Look, this is ridiculous." Sarah shook her head, trying to get ahold of the situation again. "I've sold the Ashcroft stock to LINC. Next year I'm going to start moving it, and until then, we aren't going to sell it to anyone else. By this afternoon, I'm going to have a bank draft for twenty-five percent of the contract price Dan agreed to. At the end of the contract, I'll get the balance. Then," she continued with a warning glance at Tom, who looked as though he would interrupt, "we're going to plant a few quick-sale items and more roses. I plan to take some of the money I'm getting today and install a reliable irrigation system. Then we're going to fix the heating in the greenhouses so Cecelia won't have to worry about her orchids freezing in the winter. And I may even add another greenhouse or two for common houseplants."

"You're going to sell spider plants and philodendron?" It was Tom's shocked question.

"I might!" Sarah answered with a looked that dared him to dispute her right to burn down the entire place if it pleased her to do so. "And why not? Before long, I'm going to have the money and the space and the time to work on my roses if it's the last thing I do. And if, by some act of God, this deal does fall through, I might just sell the whole damned business and take the job with Ryan and Roth. One way or the other, I'm going to stop pouring my life into maintaining a lot of darn trees that I don't care about, and I'm going to start doing what *I* want to do for a change!" She stopped abruptly, looked from one to the other of the two stony faces staring at her, and finished: "And that goes for my business *and* my personal life."

Until that moment, Sarah hadn't even realized just how true it was that she'd been living out somebody else's dream—her father's. She'd become the caretaker of a grand and glorious scheme that had had its day and was now becoming a burden to all those connected with it. Even her marriage had been a part of that scheme. Never again would she compromise her own dreams. Never again would she be somebody's pawn.

Still, as determined as she was, as she looked at the faces of her two most trusted employees and friends, she felt her mood soften. Change was coming hard to all of them.

Betty and Tom exchanged glances. Tom cleared his throat. Betty looked like she might cry.

"Look, you two," Sarah began, her tone quieter now, "you're the closest thing I've got to family. I know you're just concerned for my welfare, and I know it's hard to see Ashcroft change after all the years it's been going on without changing at all. You've got to trust that I know what I'm doing. It will work out; you'll see."

Tom pushed his hat back in a familiar gesture. "Are you really thinking of selling Ashcroft and going out west?"

Sarah smiled. "Not if I can help it. Why grow roses for somebody else if I can grow them myself?"

Tom nodded, seemingly reassured by this piece of sound logic. "That's what I've always thought," he said.

"Then you should be tickled pink that I'm working on a way to make it happen," Sarah reasoned persuasively.

Tom drew back a little, but he didn't argue.

Quietly, Betty mumbled, "I wonder what Jane would say about this . . . this young man of yours."

Sarah suppressed a laugh at the thought of Dan being described as a "young man"; the image the words conjured was of a white dinner jacket and carnations and horn-rimmed glasses. "Well," she said slowly, "I can't imagine Jane Turner not wanting me to be happy." Sarah didn't add that Jane had known very well that Sarah's marriage to her son had not been a happy one, and it had grieved Jane sorely. She'd done her best to make up for Sarah's not having a mother, but she couldn't make her son fall in love with his wife.

A short while after Betty and Tom had left her office, Dan returned. He plunked the bank draft down on Sarah's desk and then promptly lifted her out of her chair to settle there himself. He pulled her onto his lap.

"Now," he said, ignoring Sarah's wide-eyed glances at the enormous amount of money he'd just dropped so casually in front of her. "What's on the agenda for the rest of the afternoon?"

"Pesticides," Sarah answered distractedly.

"*Git* them nasty beasties!" Dan exclaimed. "Then what?"

"The bank, to put that bank draft in the night deposit."

"And then the appliance store," he added, "to buy an air conditioner."

"A what?" Sarah asked, startled.

"Darlin', I don't need any help from Mother Nature to keep you warm at night," he answered with a leering grin.

Sarah flushed. "I noticed."

"And aren't you glad?" he teased, kissing her nose. "Okay, so now our schedule is set. How about our, uh, extracurricular activities? When do we go to the Museum of Natural History? And I still haven't seen any of the memorials."

"I'll never get any work done with you around," she complained, pouting saucily.

"You're starting to sound just like Joan," he retorted.

"Your secretary and I seem to have a lot in common," Sarah noted dryly. "Maybe she can give me some advice on how to control you."

In the end, Dan had his way for the most part. Despite Betty's scowling disapproval and, later, Tom's muttered grumblings, for the rest of the week Dan followed Sarah around as she saw to the business of the nursery. And Sarah discovered that with him beside her, all that hard work wasn't like work at all. In reality, it was fun. When Dan found it impossible to drag her away from the nursery for any part of the day, he would spirit her off to the rose garden for a picnic lunch that he had taken great pains to prepare. Twice, Sarah found dinner waiting for her when she arrived home—and she tried not to groan at the sight of her kitchen in wild disorder. He was a good cook, if not the neatest one of the world.

In small ways—in *every* way—Dan became ingrained in the fabric of Sarah's life. She remembered how much at home he'd looked sitting in her father's chair that first afternoon he'd come to see the rose albums. It wasn't long before he looked at home everywhere in her house. Standing barefoot and shirtless in front of the sink, washing dishes. Sprawled on the couch with the TV on, a bowl of popcorn on his stomach—snoring. Singing Irish folk songs in front of the mirror in the morning while he shaved. Hidden behind the morning paper at the breakfast table, the only indication that he existed being the occasional turning of a page and his hand reaching around the paper for his coffee cup. Glued to the TV, swearing vehemently and loudly at an Orioles-Yankees game.

They made meals together, they cuddled on the couch and listened to music together, they took baths together in the big old-fashioned claw-footed bathtub. Most of all, they made love together.

It was idyllic. It was exactly the way Sarah thought life should be. It was exactly the way she'd always thought marriage should be . . .

That thought gave her pause and sent her head reeling back into that slightly off-balance place that she'd lived in for the most part since Dan had walked into her life. She was only vaguely aware, however, of the warning in the back of her mind that said it was too soon, that one did not fall in love and get married in less than two weeks. And if one did, then one deserved what one got! By this time, she'd grown accustomed to that little voice; she thought of it rather nostalgically, if somewhat prematurely, as the voice of her past: the voice of a staid and proper and very slow-paced existence that had had its place but had never brought her even close to being really happy. And here she was, actually ecstatic! Thus, that nagging voice was being exchanged for something else. She wasn't quite sure what the something else was; it had something to do with going after what she wanted. It had a lot to do with being happy. And, certainly, it had a lot to do with Dan Lowell.

It was Wednesday morning, when Sarah opened her eyes to find herself staring at Dan's dark, sleep-tousled head beside hers on the pillow, that she finally acknowledged what had happened. She studied his face—those incredible lashes that lay against his cheeks, the strong jaw, the sensual mouth. In that peaceful moment, the quiet voice that had been whispering in the back of her mind—for how long now?—worked its way into her consciousness. Quite suddenly and painlessly, she knew. She was in love. Completely and irrevocably. The idea filled her whole being with a sort of innocent enchantment. She'd never been in love before. It was beautiful and exciting. Magical.

Seconds later, Dan's eyes opened and met hers, and he smiled sleepily. Sarah was caught up in her feelings, and it never once occurred to her that her eyes were speaking her thoughts; certainly it never occurred to her to hide her love from him.

"Yes, I know," he whispered softly in reply to her unspoken declaration, his eyes never leaving hers.

"How did you know?" she asked, not really surprised that he did. "I only just realized it myself."

"I know because I love you," he answered simply. "I couldn't have allowed it to be true that you didn't love me too."

"You're arrogant."

"You're beautiful."

"Kiss me."

"Not until you say it."

"I love you. I love you. I love...Oh, Dan..."

When Saturday came, Sarah was exhausted after a hard week's work. Dan, however, insisted that they get dressed in something besides work clothes and go out.

Sarah lay flat on her back on her bed, where she'd fallen when they'd come in, and groaned. "All I want to do is lie here in this wonderful air-conditioned room and relax." She grinned at him hopefully.

"Absolutely not." Dan shook his head, pulling his sweat-soaked T-shirt over his head and unbuckling his belt. "We've worked for six straight days, and it's been one of the best weeks I've spent in years. But tonight we're going to eat at the Jockey Club, and then we're going to get in the elevator and go up to the eighth floor. You've had a week to get over being there on business. Sooner or later you'll have to face my world, and it might as well be tonight." His pants fell in a lump on the floor and he kicked them aside.

Sarah remained immobile. Dan stood over her, arms crossed in front of him and a determined look etching his brow. She glanced over his scantily attired form. "You know," she remarked dreamily, "if you ever get tired of building cities, you could make a living modeling men's underwear."

Dan's eyebrow shot up, and he grinned piratically. "You're not going to get out of it that easy, lady. Get your bottom off that bed and strip...*now!*"

"Why do I feel like I'm about to be sacrificed to the wolves?" she asked with a sigh.

"Come join me in the bathtub, and I'll answer that question," he replied.

By the time she was seated in the lantern-lit dining room of the Ritz-Carlton, Sarah was glad they'd come. She glanced up at the dark varnished timbers of the ceiling, from which were hung various pewter and copper pieces; she took in the warm, intimate atmosphere of the restaurant and began to think she'd been very silly not to want to spend more time there. The place was truly marvelous. Besides, Dan had to start work on Monday morning when his offices opened. They couldn't be together every day and every night as they had been. But there would be more days and nights if she were willing to come to him. For that, she'd get over her aversion to spending the night in his suite.

Sarah listened to Dan talk about his schedule over the next few weeks. He expected to walk into the offices Monday morning and find things much as he'd left them two weeks before—except that all had been moved two hundred and fifty miles south. As she listened Sarah's attention wandered. She lost track of his words and concentrated on the way his mouth curved up slightly higher on the left side when he smiled, the way his words slurred together with just a hint of brogue when he was feeling relaxed, the way they'd made love in the bathtub a few hours earlier...

"...and then I joined the Foreign Legion and have been living in India for the last fifty years."

"What?" Sarah stared at him blankly for a minute and then blushed. "Oh, Dan, I'm sorry. I didn't hear what you said."

He chuckled. "I know, but don't be sorry. I love it when you look at me like that. I just wish you'd save it for a more appropriate place."

"What were you saying?" she asked dutifully.

"It wasn't important," he said, shrugging. "Just pouring my heart out about Rosecroft and working over the details of the meetings I've got lined up this week with the builders and a multitude of other folks."

"Yes, and what else?"

"No"—he shook his head—"I'd rather sit here and give you the other half of that wicked expression you were giving me."

"You'd better not or we'll get thrown out."

"Never," he countered, as though affronted. "Look around. We aren't the only lovers here."

Sarah glanced at the crowd seated around them and realized that he could be right. There were a number of very official-looking gentlemen and a few ladies, some obviously foreign—which, in D.C., was hardly unusual. But there were also a number of other couples who looked as though they weren't aware there was anyone else in the room.

"May I suggest that we adjourn this meeting to a more convenient location?" Dan gave her a suggestive look, and Sarah nodded with a smile.

He rose from his seat, but just then a very tall and elegantly dressed woman who was passing by their table stopped suddenly. "Why, Mr. Lowell!" she exclaimed. "How delightful! I didn't know you'd arrived in town!"

Dan looked at the woman and hesitated, obviously

waiting for her to introduce herself.

"Yes, yes, I know. You don't know me." The statuesque brunette realized his confusion and hurried to explain. "I'm Emily Potsdam," she said in the rather too-friendly way, and identified herself as a columnist for a Washington paper. "I can't tell you what a pleasure it is to welcome you to the District, Mr. Lowell," she continued. "We've all been looking forward to meeting you."

"I'm flattered, Ms. Potsdam," Dan replied in a tone that indicated he couldn't have cared less.

Emily Potsdam, however, was not to be deterred. "Indeed, Mr. Lowell," she went on, "the business community is, of course, delighted to see LINC join its ranks. But I, for one, am far more interested in the *man* who stands at its helm. You've made such an interesting subject..." Ms. Potsdam had turned and caught a glimpse of Sarah as she spoke, and now she stopped and looked closer.

Sarah drew back under the scrutiny, knowing she couldn't avoid the inevitable.

"Why...yes! It *is* Sarah Turner! How utterly delightful!"

"Hello, Ms. Potsdam." Sarah smiled wanly.

"You ladies know each other?" Dan asked, clearly surprised.

"Why, I've done business with the Ashcroft Nursery for *years*!" Emily Potsdam exclaimed. "And you two are neighbors in a way, now, aren't you? Well, isn't that *nice*!"

Sarah and Dan exchanged a brief but significant look, and Dan would have found a way to hurry them out of there, but Emily Potsdam would not be given the slip that easily.

"Now, tell me, how did you two meet? Surely this isn't a business conference?"

"No, Ms. Potsdam, it is not," Dan stated flatly. "Now, if you'll excuse us..."

"Well, you must tell me how this came about," the columnist went on as though Dan hadn't spoken. "I'm sure you know, Mr. Lowell, you've left quite a few broken hearts in New York. We're dying to know more about you here down south."

"I'll bet," said Dan in a tone that barely concealed his irritation.

Emily Potsdam laughed airily, oblivious to the signs that Sarah recognized all too well. "As you might guess, we've all wondered who would be the lucky lady—or should I say ladies—to have the honor of your attention." Again that airy laugh. "You're such a colorful man, Mr. Lowell!"

Sarah watched the red rising on Dan's neck and knew that Emily Potsdam was about to see just how colorful he could be if she kept it up.

"Now, Mrs. Turner, I hope you realize what you've managed to accomplish. Imagine you snaring him right from beneath my eyes before I even knew for sure he'd arrived! You *must* tell me how the two of you—"

"Tell me, Ms. Potsdam, how is that redbud I sold you last year?" Sarah made the interruption smoothly, and she silently congratulated herself on her polite tone.

Emily Potsdam stopped in mid-sentence and looked flustered for a moment. Then she shook her head and replied, "Well, it's doing quite well, I suppose." And then, with a big smile, she turned to Dan. "Have you shown Mr. Lowell all those lovely roses? Perhaps he'll buy some for that new city of his. Is that what the two of you are talking about? But no, you said it wasn't bus—"

"You know, Ms. Potsdam, you really should come out sometime next week and look at the new red hybrid tea rose that I'm growing this year." Sarah stood gracefully and picked up her bag. "I'm sure it would do nicely in your garden. The garden club would simply love it, I'm sure." And with a conspiratorial wink, she added, "You'd be a step ahead of the others, because it's still in the experimental stage. It doesn't even have a name yet." She walked casually to Dan's side and slipped her arm through his as she added, "Next year, of course, it will be advertised all over the country, and then everybody will be wanting it. You really must come soon. Now, I know you want to get back to your dinner. We've kept you too long as it is."

"Why, no, I just—"

"It's been a pleasure meeting you, Ms. Potsdam," Dan said, grabbing the woman's hand and giving it a shake.

"I'll look for you at the nursery." Sarah smiled brightly. "If I'm not in the office, tell my assistant to find me. I'll take good care of you."

"Thank you, but—"

"Good night!" Sarah waved gaily over her shoulder as Dan ushered her briskly toward the lobby entrance, threading his way among tables and around waiters carrying trays of steaming food.

When they reached the lobby, Sarah couldn't hold back any longer. She covered her mouth with the back of her hand and giggled, glancing sideways at Dan as they made their way toward the elevators.

"Don't look at me," Dan ordered. "I don't want to laugh until I get out of sight. Chances are good she's still watching."

Suddenly, Sarah realized he was probably right. She stopped abruptly and tugged his arm to guide him toward the front door.

"In that case," she said, "we'll go out this way, I think."

"Why on earth...?" Dan looked at her in confusion and then, when he realized her intent, exclaimed, "Sarah! Don't be ridiculous! So what if she knows you went up to my suite?"

"She'll know we're...that we're lovers," Sarah pointed out, feeling the pink rise in her cheeks.

"Who cares what she knows!"

"Do you want all of Washington to know? They will. Tomorrow morning, first thing. You may be accustomed to having your name smeared all over the papers, but I'm not!"

Dan pulled her to a halt at the top of the marble stairs that led to the entrance. "So what should we do?" he asked with a sardonic twist of his mouth. "Sneak in the back entrance? Sarah this is ridiculous! I love you, and I don't care who knows it!"

"Dan, not so loud." Sarah looked around and blushed at the curious glances being cast their way by a man and woman just getting off of the elevator.

"I'll be as loud as I want!" he growled.

But Sarah was relieved that, although the timbre of his voice was deep, he was making some effort to keep it down.

"There is absolutely nothing that woman can say about me that somebody hasn't already said," Dan told her bluntly.

Sarah grumbled, "You don't know Emily Potsdam."

"She can't be any worse than Alicia Mertz, whom I've come to loathe. I lived through her, and I'll survive Emily."

"Don't bet on it," Sarah warned, and then, with a sigh of resignation, she rolled her eyes and said, "All right. If you don't care, then let's go. It's your reputation I'm trying to protect, but it's beginning to sound like there's nothing left to salvage."

Sarah took a step toward the elevator. This time it was Dan who hung back.

"Are you worried about *your* reputation?" he asked curiously.

Sarah hesitated, shook her head, and started to say no. But she couldn't. She was worried. Perhaps it was unmodern and prudish, but that was the way she'd been raised, and she couldn't help it. Sarah turned away, unable to meet his gaze.

"Sarah?" Dan brought her face back to his with a finger under her chin. "You don't really believe you're just another notch in my well-marked and *extremely* overrated belt, do you?"

Sarah saw the almost wounded look in his eyes, and her heart melted. "Oh, Dan, no. Of course, I don't believe that . . . but . . ."

"But other people will. Is that it?" he persisted, his expression no longer hurt but growing hard and determined.

"As I said," Sarah whispered, "you don't know Emily Potsdam. She can be, uh, very convincing. Look"—she straightened and managed a shaky smile—"I'm probably just being silly. Let's go on upstairs. We'll have to get up early and..."

Dan didn't move. He was studying her face very thoroughly.

"Dan...?" She looked at him questioningly.

"No way," he stated flatly. "I'm not going up there with you feeling like some crazy mix between a sacrificial virgin and a cheap whore."

Sarah's eyes widened and she started to reply angrily, but he didn't give her time to speak. Abruptly, he turned and began striding back toward the entrance to the dining room.

Sarah hesitated less than a second and then hurried to catch up.

"Dan!" she whispered urgently, tugging at his arm. "What are you doing?"

"I'm going to do what I should have done in the first place," he replied coldly. "I'm going to tell Emily Potsdam the truth. The *whole* truth."

Sarah hauled frantically at his arm, finally bringing him to a stop just before he reached the dining room. "What do you mean, you're going to tell her the truth?" she asked, panic rising in her throat.

Dan looked down at her with anger-glazed eyes. "I'm going back in there and tell her I'm madly in love with you and that we're going to be married! I'll be damned if I'll—"

"You're *what*?" Sarah's whisper cracked as her heart pounded loudly in her chest.

Dan gave her a quick, impatient look. "I'm going to tell her we're engaged," he repeated. "I won't have you wishing you could hide from the world, worrying about what people are saying, wondering whether it will affect your business. We're going to settle the thing, Sarah, and I won't argue with you about it any further!"

"But..." Sarah stared at him in shock, and her head began to reel. "Dan, are you...are you saying that we *are* going to be married? Or are you just going to tell Emily that?" She could feel herself start to tremble, her knees turning to water beneath her as she waited for his answer.

Dan opened his mouth to offer another angry volley. Then his words were choked off and the glazed look left his eyes as he registered the trembling of her hand on his arm and the fearful, vulnerable look in her gaze. Instantly, his whole countenance changed, softened, begged her forgiveness. "Sarah..." He tossed his head back for a moment and squeezed his eyes shut tightly. The look he next gave her was one of self-disgust and great tenderness. "Sarah, darling, I'm sorry. I've been thinking about it so much myself, it seemed like I *must* already have asked you! I've said the words a hundred times in my dreams. I've been afraid of pushing you too fast, too soon..." His searing gaze and husky voice pleaded as he asked, "Am I pushing you, Sarah? Can you possibly be ready to say yes, you'll marry me?"

No, she wasn't ready, she thought as she stood transfixed by the look in his eyes, both of them oblivious now to the curious glances they were getting from passersby. Yes, it was too fast. And yes, her head was spinning totally out of control, And yes, she was afraid that so much happiness could not possibly be real. But refusing Dan was unthinkable; she'd learned that much. It had been hard the first times they'd kissed; after they'd made love, it had become, quite literally, impossible. Still, a nagging little suspicion goaded her to ask. "You're not just doing this to spite the Alicia Mertzes and Emily Potsdams of the world, are you?"

"You're an idiot," Dan said in tender amusement.

"I had to ask," Sarah told him, flushing pink with embarrassment.

"You're also the sexiest, most delicious woman I've ever known—which, according to Alicia Mertz, is saying quite a lot."

"You're insatiable."

"You're mine."

"Dan?"

"Hmm?"

"I think we'd better go upstairs now."

The look he gave her made a mockery of innocence. "Why, Sarah! What about Ms. Potsdam? Shouldn't we tell her the news first?"

Sarah shook her head slowly. "Emily can wait. I can't."

Dan chuckled as he allowed himself to be led toward their escape route to the upper floors. "Can I assume that this means you intend to make an honest man of me?"

"What do you think?" Sarah gave him a sidelong look as they entered the elevator.

Dan sighed as the door whooshed closed. "It's awful to have to disappoint your fans. Emily—Alicia—gee. When I'm safely married away, maybe I'll cut that old belt of mine in half and send them each a piece to remember me by."

Sarah's head turned slowly and she met his teasing look with one that was blatantly seductive in its hot sensuality. Her hand reached out and pulled back one side of his dark blue jacket as her eyes dropped to focus on his waist. Then her gaze dropped still lower and she said huskily, "Honey, it isn't your *belt* they want. And what they want they can't have, because you just gave it to me—for keeps."

That night, Sarah made certain that Dan understood the terms of their contract. And Dan, having lost more than just his belt, thought it wise not to argue. Very sensibly, he signed—with a bold and masterful stroke—on the dotted line.

- *6* -

IT WAS WORSE than Sarah had expected. Much worse.

NEW YORK TYCOON-PLAYBOY COURTS LOCAL BUSINESS— Sarah groaned at the headline of Emily Potsdam's column. Her eyes scanned the article for the third time, hoping it wasn't really as bad as it had first appeared. But it was.

That handsome darling of the New York jet set, Daniel Lowell, has moved his operations south— in more ways than one. LINC opens its offices in the District on Monday morning, but the president and chairman of the board isn't waiting for office hours to acquaint himself with the female population in the District—and thereabouts. If the commercial landscapers in the northern suburbs of D.C. are panting for a chance to bid on the contract for LINC's new town, they'd better take a long, *cold* drink of water and look elsewhere. The competition looks fierce in the lovely form of Ms. Sarah Turner of Ashcroft Nursery. Yes, Mr. Lowell has been getting to know his neighbors. He and Ms. Turner made a handsome couple last night at the Jockey Club—the dining room of the Ritz-Carlton, where Mr. Lowell is staying. The looks being exchanged across the table where Mr. Lowell and Ms. Turner were seated—and later as they got on the elevator—might lead one to believe there was love in the air. Indeed, it looks to me as though the bidding is closed. Sorry to disappoint you fellas, but it seems your shrubs have the wrong sort of hormones. But oh, dear, the real loss will be felt among all those ladies who have been waiting anxiously to see if Mr. Lowell lives up to his reputation. Well, take heart, ladies: He's never been known to stay in one place very long . . .

Sarah laid the paper down on her desk. She felt sick. How could the woman get away with it? Weren't there laws to prevent such disgusting prattle from being printed? And what in the world was Sarah going to do about it?

She was mulling over various possible acts of violence that could be perpetrated against Emily Potsdam when Betty walked in. Sarah looked up, surprised to see her office manager at work on a Sunday.

The older woman came over to Sarah's desk, took one look at the paper lying before her, and said, "So, you've seen it. Hmph! It's disgusting! I hope now you see why I tried to warn you—"

"Dan and I are getting married, Betty." Sarah interrupted quietly.

There was a silence; then: "Married? You're going to *marry* him?"

Sarah looked up from the newsprint to meet Betty's horrified look directly. "That's right. He loves me, and I love him. People in love often marry. It's really not that uncommon."

Betty blinked in confusion. Sarah could see that she

clearly hadn't been anticipating this turn of events. It was almost funny to see the older woman thrown into such a state.

And then the confusion cleared. "You had better watch yourself, miss," Betty warned. "Maybe he does love you, but then again, maybe there's more here than he's saying."

Sarah's eyes narrowed and she spoke in an ominously quiet tone. "Are you saying that Emily Potsdam is right?"

"That Potsdam woman ought to be . . . Oooooh, what I'd like to do to her!" Betty's wrinkled face clenched in anger, and then she wagged a finger in Sarah's direction. "But that man! Now, he's something else again. He's saying he loves you—and maybe he does—but I'm telling you, Sarah, you ought to slow down and *think*—"

"I know, I know," Sarah cut in wearily. Suddenly she knew she had to get out of the office, away from Betty and Emily Potsdam and everything else. A great longing to see her garden came over her, and she pushed herself back from her desk abruptly.

"Dan's on his way over here," she said, rising quickly and walking toward the door. "When he comes, tell him I'm in the garden."

And without a backward glance at her scowling assistant, Sarah ran out.

She jumped into the small pickup and bounced down the dirt road to the back of the property, heedless of the bright morning sunshine or the beating she was giving the vehicle she drove. The truck ground to a halt outside the garden; then Sarah was out the door and running to the garden gate, flinging it open and pulling it closed behind her.

She collapsed for a moment against it, drinking in the sight of the undisturbed beauty around her. The garden was still. It was early and the sun hadn't yet passed over the old flowering crab apple. A slight breeze stirred, and she was hit with a wave of heavenly smells from the musk rose that grew by the gate. She looked at the white

petals, thinking how plain they were, while they pro-
duced such a treasure chest of fragrance. She reached
out and broke off a cluster of six or seven blooms and
then began walking slowly toward the tree in the center
of the garden. There she sat down on the thick and
slightly-too-long grass, crossing her legs and idly fingering the stems of the flowers she held in her lap.

Why was she letting Emily Potsdam—and Betty,
too—ruin everything? Why was she allowing her own
irrational fears and doubts to be fed by their totally
off-the-wall accusations? She knew she was guilty of
letting it get to her, and it angered her further that she
should be so weak and malleable; why couldn't she just
laugh in their faces, secure in the knowledge that Dan
loved her and wanted her to be his wife?

The answer came unbidden and unwanted. She let
them bother her because she *did* worry that, perhaps,
they were right. Perhaps Dan really did see their relationship as a business deal—despite all evidence to the
contrary. After all, he'd come to Ashcroft on business
in the first place; would he ever really separate that fact
from his view of her?

And even if he could—even if her fears were, as she
suspected, totally irrational—would the rest of the world
ever see their relationship as anything but a very convenient arrangement? Emily Potsdam had gone a long
way toward sealing their fate in that regard. Marriage
might deprive Emily of ammunition for waging war
against Dan's reputation, but it wouldn't help either Dan
or herself as far as their businesses were concerned. If
anything, their getting married would make matters worse.
When it was discovered—as it soon would be—that
Ashcroft Nursery was, indeed, going to landscape Rosecroft, the business community would be certain that
Emily had been right in her assessment. There would be
all sorts of talk of favoritism and unfair business practices. Of course, LINC had a right to choose whomever
it wanted to do the landscaping, but all the building
contracts had been decided in competitive bidding. Peo-

ple would wonder why the landscaping hadn't been done
similarly. Commercial landscaping was a cutthroat business. The competition was brutal. Hank Tyler and Robert
Barron, to name just two local landscapers, would be
outraged that they hadn't been given a shot at the contract.

Sarah tossed the rose petals she held onto the grass
and sighed. She hadn't done anything wrong. Dan hadn't
done anything unethical. But it would look very bad to
everyone else, no matter what they said or did now. Their
only option would be either to stop seeing one another
entirely or to call off their business deal. Sarah hated the
thought of having to return to Dan the money he'd ad-
vanced her on the contract; it meant going back to square
one in her ongoing dilemma about the nursery. But the
thought of not seeing Dan, of not being able to love
him—of sacrificing her own happiness and his—was
unthinkable. Dan, she knew, would never give in to such
pressure, and he would be livid if he thought she'd even
considered it. Yet, Sarah knew that the gossip wouldn't
stop. The opinions of Emily Potsdam and others would
continue to be bandied about, creating the hint of doubt
in everyone's mind that she and Dan had married not for
love but for mutual gain. The idea was preposterous, but
wouldn't it nonetheless cast an unfavorable light on their
relationship? Could love survive such pressure?

Before she could begin to answer the question, the
gate opened and Dan slipped inside. He had the newspaper in his hand, and when he latched and locked the
gate behind him and walked over and sat down on the
grass beside her, Sarah said gloomily, "I left the office
to get *away* from that!"

"Sarah," Dan began urgently, angrily, "this doesn't
change a thing." And with great perceptiveness, as though
he'd been there reading all of her thoughts, he went on
to say, "Let them think whatever they want. You and I
are getting married. To hell with them! I'm not marrying
you for your damed trees, but there's no reason on earth
why it's not perfectly legitimate for me to buy them."

"Maybe it would be better if you didn't," Sarah suggested weakly.

"No! Dammit! I will not be told by some gossip columnist how to run my business *or* my love affairs! And you won't go back on our contract just because it might hurt some landscapers' feelings!"

"It's not just their feelings," Sarah protested, looking at his angry countenance, her green eyes wide and pleading. "You're just starting out here in the business community. This is a horrible way to begin. You should be building goodwill and good public relations, not doing things to make people think you conduct your business deals . . ." She trailed off, realizing what she'd been about to say.

"In the bedroom," Dan finished curtly. "It won't be the first time I've been accused of it. If even half of what's been written about me were true, I'd have lost the company years ago. Sarah"—he took her shoulders and made her look at him—"don't you do this. I can see you thinking about foolish things. I'm not going to give you up. And I'm not going to have Rosecroft planted with anything but what I've already bought! I want you *and* the damned trees, and I'm not going to let anything get in my way!"

Sarah's eyes searched his face. "Oh, Dan . . ." She sobbed brokenly, and quite unexpectedly she found tears spilling down her cheeks.

His look softened and he gathered her into his arms. "Ah, darlin', there now," he crooned softly, "You know I love you, and what does it matter what anyone else thinks?"

She shook her head against his shoulder. "I'm sorry, it's just that I'm so confused. I have to keep reminding myself that it really is me you want. You . . . you don't understand about . . ." She sobbed against him, unable to finish the thought.

"About the only other man in your life until I came along?" he asked gently.

Sarah drew back, startled.

Dan smiled. "Give me some credit, Sarah. I know you were married to Bill Turner. And I know you *never* mention him—not even in passing. You don't speak ill of him, but you also don't talk about anything the two of you ever did together that was pleasant. You might have been sparing my feelings, but I think it's more likely there's another reason."

"There wasn't anything we did together to talk about," she admitted with stark honesty. "Nothing bad—nothing pleasant—just nothing."

"You grew up together, didn't you?" he pursued.

"And we got married." She nodded.

"And not very much changed just because you did," he continued, his guesses closer to the truth than Sarah would ever have dreamed possible. "It was a very convenient business arrangement, wasn't it? Obviously, the proper thing to do. Ashcroft stayed very correctly in the family, and life went on with the future well secured. And whether or not you were happy was totally irrelevant."

"Bill wasn't happy either," Sarah whispered, as though realizing it for the first time. "Neither of us was. Neither of us ever complained or even came close to admitting the truth to each other. We just went on living in the same house I'd always lived in, going to work together each morning . . . going to sleep in the same bed each night." She shivered with cold at the memories of all those empty nights and began to wonder how Bill had ever lived through them. But then, he hadn't. "Not once did we talk about the simple fact that we had never wanted to be married in the first place." She looked at Dan, startled at the thoughts that now seemed to tumble into place in her mind. "It ruined everything! We'd been friends all our lives! Bill was older than I was, but he'd played with me and watched out for me, and we grew up being *friends*. I adored him and would have done anything in the world for him, but I was never, ever, in love with him!"

Sarah took a great gulp of air between the sobs and

violent clenching of her stomach. She stared straight ahead, her eyes wide open and the tears glittering in them. "When we got married," she continued bitterly, "it ruined everything. I felt guilty that I couldn't love him like a wife should love her husband. I wonder . . . I wonder if it was like that for him. Maybe he felt as guilty as I did. It didn't seem that he'd ever tried to love me, but maybe it was just that he couldn't fall in love with me any more than I could fall in love with him. Oh, God! When I think of the years we both wasted, trying to make something work that never should have happened in the first place . . . !"

Dan listened and let her rage and tremble with all those years' worth of built-up indignation at the people who'd encouraged her to throw her life away, who never questioned whether it was good for her or Bill—knew only that it was convenient and pleasing to them that the two should be married. And Sarah shook with fury at herself for having played the victim so well. Finally she fell into Dan's arms, racked with sobs of bitterness and grief; she cried for herself, but mostly she cried for Bill in a way that she never had when he died. She'd spent so much time resenting him as her husband that she'd never allowed herself to feel the loss of him as a friend. And it seemed as though, once she'd gotten started, she would never stop. It was such an unbearable relief finally to speak the truth, to see herself and others for what they had really been and not to try to pretend any longer.

At last, when her crying had subsided, Dan pulled a handkerchief from his pocket, wiped her cheeks with it, and then handed it to her. She took it from him with shaking fingers and blew her nose. When she was able to speak again, she ran her hand back through her hair, pushing it back off her face, and looked at him.

"I'm . . . I'm sorry you've had to listen to this. It's been so hard to keep telling myself that your loving me doesn't have anything to do with . . . with *business*." She spat the word as though it were the foulest oath one could utter.

"Tell me, Sarah," he began in a gentle, questioning tone, "does the way I make love to you even remotely resemble the way your husband did?"

Sarah blushed to the bottoms of her feet and looked away. "Don't even suggest it," she said quietly. "There's no comparison."

"Have you ever had a moment's doubt when I'm holding you in my arms, or when we're lying together, making love, that I love you for yourself and nothing more?"

She shook her head. "No. I've never doubted you. Not consciously. But I guess I've doubted myself. I've been afraid my instincts are all screwed up, that I wouldn't know what was good for me even if I had it right there in my hand." She paused, swallowed hard, and whispered, "Betty hasn't helped. And now this awful article..."

"You've had a time of it, with the Bettys and Mrs. Potsdams of the world, haven't you?" Dan remarked dryly. And then his look grew amused, "I can see that I'm going to be busy keeping your instincts on the right track."

Sarah turned her head to meet his gaze and caught her breath. His tone had been light, but the message was clear. And in her vulnerable, raw state, she suddenly found herself throbbing with need for him. She wanted him to take her; she wanted to feel the strong, hard maleness of him possessing her.

As Dan watched he saw her face change and read the look for what it was. Her parted lips, the shimmering green of her eyes, her whole body, radiated a potent sensuality that was the essence of woman. His own essence leaped out to match hers. Instantly, without a word being spoken, without so much as the lightest touch of her flesh and his, the air was filled with the power of their mating, the pure energy of male and female meeting and blending in a look shared between them that was as ancient and as timeless as life itself.

When the look demanded that they fulfill the promise it made, Dan's arm tightened around Sarah's shoulders.

Gently he laid her back on the grass. Then placing just the lightest of kisses on her parted lips, he began removing her clothes. The white cotton blouse opened under his fingers and was pushed down her arms. He lifted her a little and took it out from underneath; only when he'd laid it carefully aside did he come back to unsnap the jeans she wore, his fingers perfectly steady as he lowered the zipper and pulled them down off her hips. He lifted first one foot, then the other, until her legs were bare. The jeans he placed alongside the blouse. Then both of his arms were around her, unclasping her bra and pulling it off until the white, perfect globes underneath it were revealed to his impassioned gaze. His fingers lingered just a moment on her waist before he took hold of the scrap of blue lace she still wore, and then that, too, was gone.

When Sarah reached for the buttons of his shirt, he pushed her hands aside. "Uh-uh." He shook his head in denial. "You're just a lovely white rose." And he reached down beside her to pick up the cluster of musk roses she'd broken off earlier. "Your only purpose is to be beautiful and smell sweet. See?" He held the roses for her inspection, and she saw as he pointed that a honeybee was clinging to the petals of one blossom. Dan brushed the bee away, saying, "You see? It's your garden. Your lover comes to you."

And then, one by one, he began to pluck the petals off the musk roses and place the snowy white teardrops delicately on her throat, her shoulders, her breasts. Sarah was mesmerized, hardly dared to breath. Her skin tingled everywhere that he touched her with the fragrant blossoms. Slowly, Dan continued his ritual, leaving a trail of petals across her waist and the satin smooth skin of her belly, placing one petal over her navel and then a trail of them downward and across one thigh close to where it lay pressed against the other.

The last blossom he left whole, but plucked if off the cluster and placed it carefully on the golden triangle that covered the center of her womanhood. Then his hand slid between her legs and parted her thighs ever so slightly, holding them there for a moment as though to say he wanted her ready for him.

He rose to his feet and, just as deliberately and as slowly, he removed his own clothing. His eyes never left hers and she watched him, entranced. First, his shirt went to join her clothes. She stared at the broad expanse of muscle and dark, curling hair and lightly tanned flesh. The flat nipples in the middle of those swirls of hair were dark, hard little nubs. The muscles of his neck and shoulders tensed as he undid his belt, and the zipper of his jeans sounded loud in the stillness. He shoved his pants off his narrow hips, his brief shorts with them, and in one smooth movement he kicked aside the heap of clothes he'd so carefully made.

And then he stood for a moment quite still, and his eyes raked over her. His whole body was tense and pulsing with pure male force—a force that was possessive and bold and utterly arrogant. Sarah trembled under his look until the petals covering her trembled too. She felt intensely vulnerable, as though she had no choice but to lay there—open and exposed to the warm air and filtered sunshine—and let him come to her as he would.

Dan dropped to the ground beside her. Very slowly, with infinite control, his mouth began to move across her, following the path he'd only just made with the roses. Kissing, biting, licking away the petals he'd placed on her throat and across her shoulders, his mouth blazed an unrelenting path of fire from her right shoulder to her left breast. A gleaming white velvety petal covered the peak of the soft mound, and this he enclosed with his lips, then his teeth, gentle, encasing the throbbing, swelling peak with the fragile fabric. Sarah moaned from deep inside as he loosened his hold and licked the petal aside to suck hungrily on the exposed bud.

His mouth left her breast and she felt unspeakably shaken. It was frightening, this deliberate eroticism. It stripped her of whatever vestiges of pretense there were left, of whatever defense there was to be found in more conventional lovemaking, no matter how passionate it might be. The act in which they were engaged was pure and untainted; they might have been the first two, the only two, lovers ever to have loved. It was an act so free of constraint and guilt and worldliness that it brought tears to Sarah's eyes. And they flowed unchecked as she lay compliant, accepting, and completely open as Dan worshiped her body with his, his touch and his eyes speaking to her with complete adoration and uninhibited love.

Traveling downward to pause over the gentle curve of her belly and the petals he had placed there, his tongue teased circles around her navel and left her gasping for breath. One by one, he removed the white pieces from the tender flesh of her right thigh, licking at the scent the petals had left to linger on her skin. With one hand, he spread apart her thighs, exposing the very core of her to the mercilessness of his blue-fire gaze.

And then, with one caressing look along the length of her body to meet her passion-drugged gaze of wonderment, his head lowered until his face was buried in that complete rose he'd placed upon the bed of her femininity. Exactly as though she herself were that blossom and he the tireless, persistent bee in search of its sweet golden nectar, he opened his mouth and tasted of her in the most exquisitely erotic way imaginable.

Sarah could neither stop him nor urge him on—could only let him take her in the precise way he intended. Her legs shook uncontrollably; the silent tears turned to sobs of unbearable pleasure and joy. Her breath came in tiny gasps and moans that didn't stop even when his mouth finally left her. She was aware only of a deep, yearning, aching void inside of her that only he could create, only he could fill and make right.

And as though he'd called to her, she opened her eyes to find him leaning over her. There was yet another of those pieces of fragrant white gold held between his teeth. He lowered his head until the petal brushed her lips. Gently, he rubbed it across her quivering mouth. And then, turning his head slightly, he let the petal fall. When his mouth came back to hers, his tongue traced the outline of her lips, and she could hear him breathing deeply of the musky scent. He nibbled gently, teasingly, as though he were coaxing her mouth to open just as he had opened the petals of her womanhood. Her lips moved to caress his, longed for his full possession. Only when a sob escaped her and another tear slid out of the corner of her eye did he meet her longing with his own.

In one devastating moment, he took her. She gasped and he swallowed the sound with his mouth. Her flesh encased him, welcomed him, quivered beneath and around him. He drank from her and filled her, taking everything from her she had to give and leaving the aching void inside of her saturated with every fiber of his being.

The climax of the storm came upon them quickly and with such vilolent force that, in the end, they were both taken, both caught up in something far more powerful than either of them could have created alone. The earth beneath them seemed to shake, and everything went black until all that was left was trembling flesh and the smell of musk.

Sarah didn't know how long she slept, but realized it must have been quite a while when she was awakened by the sensation of raindrops falling on her nude body. Dan lay facedown beside her, his arm thrown across her, one hand covering her breast. Up through the heavy-laden boughs of the crab apple she could see that the sky was nearly black. A flash of lightning skittered across the darkness to the west, to be followed a few seconds later by the distant rumbling of thunder.

Sarah rolled carefully to her side and, placing her hand on Dan's shoulder, shook him gently.

"Dan . . .? Wake up."

"Hmm?" he grumbled, raising his head to look at her through half-closed eyes.

"Dan, it's raining," she said regretfully.

He opened his eyes wide, blinked, and then rolled slowly onto his back to stare at the sky. "We won't get very wet if we stay under the tree," he pointed out, his voice low as though he were afraid words would break the spell they'd made.

"You don't think we ought to go?" she asked tentatively.

"Do you?"

She shook her head. Their eyes met in silent accord. There would be no more work that day. They had turned that ordinary Sunday morning into something quite different, and they had neither the desire nor the will to change it back into something ordinary. All they wanted was to be together—to dream, maybe to talk.

And so the two lovers waited out the storm, wrapped safe in the cocoon of the enchanted garden. When it was over, they put on their damp clothing and wandered back to the pickup Sarah had left outside the gate. Dan's car they would worry about later. Not wanting to pass the office, they took the long way back to Sarah's house through the nursery. When they got there, she took the phone off the hook and they forgot that the rest of the world existed.

Sarah went to sleep that night honestly believing for the first time in many, many years that happiness was possible and that dreams, no matter how tarnished and abused, really could come true.

- 7 -

Monday morning saw Sarah's life return to something resembling normalcy—not that she was pleased about that fact. Dan left early to be at his offices by eight. She went about the business of running her nursery, which entailed almost the same amount of work as it always had, despite the fact that she didn't have any stock to sell. Dan may have bought it, but she had to keep it alive until it was moved. However, her nursery sales helpers and Tom were telling customers that they were out of stock on all nursery items until further notice. And so there were no sales to handle.

The greenhouses, of course, were still a concern, and Sarah immediately turned her attention to the much-needed repairs to be made there. A morning conference with Cecelia Appleby found Cecelia beaming at the news that she would have a new heating system and new workbenches and new sprayers for pesticides and anything else it would take to make the greenhouses absolutely top-rate. She told Cecelia to hire herself an assistant manager and to take some much-deserved vacation time herself. And Sarah finished by saying that Cecelia should plan to start stocking the greenhouses with something besides exotic, hard-to-care for plants, and that she should include plants that would grow for even the worst of gardeners. Cecelia didn't like that part. Sarah was pleasant but firm. The conference ended with Cecelia feeling she'd gotten most of what she'd been asking for, even if she didn't like the price she'd had to pay. Philodendrons! Bah!

Then Sarah turned her attention to the irrigation system. A call to Jenkins Systems confirmed plans for the irrigation company to install whatever new parts were necessary to make the system work reliably.

Sarah spent the afternoon in the fields, fussing over her experimental roses, taking notes on their progress and laying plans for crossings she wanted to try. She returned to the office to find that Dan had called three times while she was out.

"He was quite indignant about it, too," Betty told her. "Acted like I was supposed to go fetch you for him."

"Was it important?" Sarah asked, walking toward her office door.

"How was I supposed to know? He called three times, didn't he? Must have something to say."

Sarah closed the door behind her, sat back in her chair, and propped her feet up on the wooden desk. Then she looked at the slip of paper Dan had given her with his new office phone number on it and dialed.

"LINC Corporation. Joan Avery speaking." The woman's voice was low, husky, and very pleasant.

"Is Mr. Lowell there?" Sarah asked. "This is Sarah Turner calling."

"Ah! Ms. Turner! He's been trying to reach you all afternoon. He's in a meeting just now with the vice-president and planning committee, but he told me to tell you not to expect to see him until very late. If he's unable to make it at all, he'll call you when he gets home."

"Oh," Sarah said, her disappointment communicating itself very clearly over the phone.

The other woman laughed softly. "I'm sorry, but it's been an extremely busy day."

"Oh, no!" Sarah exclaimed, "I mean, *I*'m sorry for taking the news so badly. You must have all had a trying day. And I understand the rest of the week doesn't look much better."

"You're right about that," Joan agreed. "I'm afraid Dan's schedule looks like it was made for three people. He wasn't happy about it this morning, and he said you would probably be even less pleased, if all that is any consolation."

There was a distinct question in Joan's voice—one that asked, what gave Sarah the right to be upset about Dan's schedule?—and Sarah didn't know how to respond. What had Dan told his secretary? Well, whatever he had told Joan, it wasn't Sarah's place to tell her anything at all.

"Well, thank you, Ms. Avery," Sarah said after a brief pause. "Tell Dan I called and . . . well, just tell him I called."

"Please call me Joan. I expect we'll be speaking to one another quite a bit."

"Thank you," Sarah said automatically. She did like the woman; at least her voice was warm and mellow-sounding—friendly. "And my name is Sarah," she added, realizing Joan had called Dan by his first name as well. "Tell Dan that . . . well, that whatever he needs to do tonight is fine with me."

"I'll tell him, and I promise to make it sound less like a lie than you just did."

It was close to eleven o'clock that night when Dan finally called.

"Sarah, darlin', I'm sorry. I just got home and I haven't even had dinner yet. I'm starved—and exhausted."

"Hmm . . . What?" Sarah mumbled sleepily, the phone dangling loosely near her ear. She'd waited until ten and then had gone to bed. Dan's call had awakened her and she was still a little disoriented.

"Are you in bed?" he asked in a rough version of his rich baritone.

"Uh-huh," she answered.

"Are you naked?"

"Uh-huh."

"Sarah, let me take a quick shower and drive out."

"Dan eat something and go to bed, for heaven's sake," Sarah advised. She was a little more awake now, but he sounded dead tired. "We've seen each other every day for the past two weeks almost," she continued. "It won't kill us to miss a day or two." She was actually pleased that she sounded so convincing.

"Speak for yourself," he growled, and then added with a sigh, "But I'm afraid we may have no choice. Did Joan tell you what my schedule is like this week?"

"She did. She said there should be three of you."

"Six, at least. I've got breakfast, lunch, and dinner meetings every day, and meetings in between. The worst should be over by the end of next week. I guess I should have expected to pay the piper for having disappeared for two weeks. Apparently, the world really doesn't turn without me, and I might need three whole days just to go through the stack of papers that require my signature."

"It must be nice to feel needed," Sarah said sympathetically.

"Yeah, like penicillin... *Sarah!*" He shouted her name so suddenly that Sarah's heart leaped.

"What is it?" she exclaimed.

"I almost forgot the most important thing! God, I must be tired! The planning committee accepted the landscape contract without even batting an eye. They think it's just dandy, and Leonard will be in touch with you sometime soon to work our the specific written agreement."

"Dan, that's wonderful!" Sarah leaned up on one elbow, having fully awakened upon hearing his news. She was surprised to find how truly relieved she felt—hadn't been entirely aware she was worried. Still, even though

Dan had made it official by paying her the twenty-five percent, it was nice to know it was really all going to go exactly as he'd said it would.

"Who is Leonard?" she asked curiously.

"Leonard Patterson. He's in the legal department at LINC. Leonard writes contracts. Sarah?"

"Hmm?"

"What kind of engagement ring do you want?"

"Of all the questions at a time like this!"

"Would you be upset if it wasn't a diamond? I want to give you an emerald, to match your eyes."

"Only if it's got aquamarines in it to match yours." She giggled. "Not that they'd come close to the real thing."

"Sarah?"

"Hmm?"

"Don't you think we should make some kind of announcement—I'm dying to tell people, and if I have to wait until I can get to a jeweler, I'll go nuts."

"Of course it's all right!" She laughed. "Tell the world."

"Good. I'll call Emily Potsdam first thing tomorrow morning."

Sarah didn't laugh at the mention of the woman's name. "It will do her good to get some honest-to-God facts straight from the source for a change," she said at last.

"You could be right," he agreed. And then Sarah heard him yawn.

"Goodnight, Dan," she said.

"Are you going to make me hang up?" he asked forlornly.

"Good night, Dan. I love you." Sarah smiled and waited.

Dan sighed in resignation. "I love you, too. I'll call you tomorrow."

"Don't make promises your secretary may have to keep," Sarah warned.

"Don't question my sincerity at this hour of the night. Besides, Joan's used to it. She's been keeping promises for me for years. And," he added firmly, "I intend to keep this promise myself."

"Go to sleep."

"All right. I love you."

"I love you too." Sarah nearly giggled at how ridiculous it was to be carrying on this way.

"Good night, Sarah."

"Good *night,* Dan!" she insisted.

There was a long pause. And then: "You hang up first."

"Daniel Lowell! You are a thirty-nine-year-old, highly successful businessman—not a fifteen-year-old in the throes of your first crush! You hang up that phone! Next thing you'll be asking me to count to three and hang up with you!"

"Would you?"

Sarah couldn't help it. She laughed delightedly. Then she said very tenderly, "I love you, and I'll talk to you tomorrow."

"Okay, sweetheart. Bye." This time he really did hang up.

Sarah went to sleep and dreamed about emeralds and diamonds and aquamarines that kept turning into a pair of sky-blue eyes.

By Wednesday, Sarah was really missing Dan and finally decided it was silly to lie in bed at night and miss him when she could just as easily drive into town and wait for him to come home. She wished she'd thought to ask him for a key for just such an occasion, because it would have been nice to surprise him. But she was unable to think of a way around the hotel and couldn't quite imagine talking them into letting her in. Then she remembered Joan Avery and thought it might be worth a try.

"LINC Corporation. This is Ms. Avery speaking."

"Joan? This is Sarah Turner."

"Hi, Sarah! What a week!"

"From what I hear, you're right."

"He's a monster and I wish you'd do something about it," Joan continued in a commiserating tone. "By the way, I want you to know that Dan found three minutes yesterday between his board meeting and press conference to tell me the news. I think it's just wonderful. I've never seen him so happy about anything. My best wishes to both of you."

"Thank you," Sarah said, and meant it. It was good to hear a positive reaction to her getting married when all she'd gotten from Betty and Tom were dubious looks, as though they'd believe it when they saw it. "I'm glad Dan told you, Joan," she continued. "Actually, I was wondering how to ask you this, but now that you know, it's a little easier."

"What's up?" Joan asked.

"Is there any way I can get into Dan's suite at the Ritz-Carlton without him knowing? I want to be there tonight and thought it would be nice to surprise him." It embarrassed her nearly to death to ask, but then, desperate situations called for desperate measures.

"Sure!" Joan said easily, and added, "I'll call the hotel and tell them to expect you. The manager knows me. What time will you be going?"

Sarah made the arrangements and hung up the phone, feeling better than she had in days. Just as she was about to leave the office to go get ready to leave, the phone rang again. Betty had gone home, and so Sarah answered.

"Ashcroft Nursery."

"I'd like to speak to Sarah Turner, please." An unfamiliar man's voice sounded pleasantly across the line.

"This is she," Sarah responded.

"Ms. Turner, this is Joe Miles of Miles Industries. You may not remember, but I met you several years ago just after your father died when I was working on some building along Route 208."

"I remember," Sarah replied and frowned slightly, trying to guess what a land developer could possibly want with her.

She didn't have to wait long to find out. "I understand

you're going to be getting rid of all your stock over the course of the next few years," Mr. Miles began, tentatively enough to indicate to Sarah that he wasn't quite sure of his facts.

"I don't know where you heard that, Mr. Miles," she replied, "but yes, it's true that I've sold the nursery stock. The contract hasn't been made public, however."

"I was afraid I was jumping the gun a little," he admitted apologetically. "I was anxious to talk with you before anyone else got a chance. I'll admit that, if the story is true, I'd very much like to know if you're planning to sell the property, Ms. Turner."

"Was that what you heard?" Sarah sat down at her desk, disturbed that the gossip was already picking up steam.

"I heard that you'd sold the stock to LINC Corporation, and I took the chance that you might be thinking of selling the land and getting out of the business altogether."

"I'm afraid you're mistaken, Mr. Miles," Sarah said firmly. "I have no intention of selling the Ashcroft property. The only thing that's going to be going are the trees and most of the roses. And if anyone else tells you differently, he or she is lying."

Joe Miles apologized for any inconvenience and let her know in no uncertain terms that he'd be interested anytime she changed her mind. Sarah hung up the phone and wondered if she'd have to ward off many other such calls in the future...

She had no problem at the hotel, and managed not to blush as she met the manager who personally showed her up to Dan's suite.

Sarah had no idea what time Dan would be coming home; and so, when she looked at her watch and saw that it was seven-thirty, she decided she'd better hurry. He'd called her after ten the previous two nights, but there was no way of knowing when he might get home early. She ran water in the enormous marble bathtub and took a hot bath. Then she put on the wicked-looking negligee she'd found at Bloomingdale's on the way into town. It was black and sheer, with tiny straps and a slit up one side to her hip.

Then she called room service and ordered a bottle of champagne. When it arrived, she pulled a terry robe out of Dan's closet to answer the door. Smiling bravely at the valet, she took the stand and bucket and carried them from the living room, through the double oak doors, and into the bedroom. Setting the stand by the doorway, she wiped the bucket dry on the bottom and placed it on the sumptuous rust-and-cream-colored spread at the foot of the four-poster bed. Then she climbed into bed herself, opened the book she'd brought, and prepared to wait.

At ten-fifteen she heard the door open. There was a pause, and then it clicked shut. She knew he'd see the light coming through the partially open bedroom doors the minute he walked in. The footsteps were slow as he crossed the living room and stopped. Sarah couldn't see him, but she sensed his presence. It puzzled her greatly when, instead of appearing in the doorway, she heard him turn and cross the room. She was starting to get worried, and was just about to make sure that it really was Dan who'd come in, when she heard the bathroom door open and click shut. She'd shut the door on the bedroom side, and it startled her further when she heard the lock being turned from the inside. She frowned. And then the sound of running water came through the closed door. At that, she smiled and relaxed once more.

Fifteen minutes later the door opened and he stood freshly shaven, his hair still damp, dressed in a dark blue silk robe tied around his middle so that it gaped open slightly above the belt.

"Good evening," he said smoothly. "I'm sorry to have kept you waiting, but I'm afraid I was delayed over the small matter of a wild goose."

Sarah looked at him blankly, hardly able to pay attention to what he was saying. Why were they talking? "Wild goose?" she said weakly.

"Uh-huh." He nodded, walking slowly toward her,

stopping at the foot of the bed to pick up the bottle of champagne, wrap the towel around the neck, and pop the cork. Pouring a glass for each of them, he moved the bucket to the stand that Sarah had left by the door and walked around to sit beside her on the bed. He handed her one glass, saying, "While you've been sitting here looking ravishing and good enough to eat, I've been driving like a maniac..."

"Out to my place," she groaned as she realized what he was going to say.

"And then back again," Dan finished with a sigh.

"I should have told you." She looked at him sorrowfully.

"You shouldn't have done anything but exactly what you did," he corrected. "I should have called. I just never thought you'd come."

"Well, we *could* spend the rest of the night apologizing to each other," she suggested, raising one brow.

"What sort of apology did you have in mind?" he asked with a crooked smile.

"The same sort you did," she replied.

"You'd better drink that champagne, because it's all you'll get. I don't plan to let you up for air until morning."

"Have you eaten dinner yet?"

"I'm just about to."

The next morning they ordered a huge breakfast through room service, and Sarah waited in bed while Dan answered the door. He rolled the cart into the bedroom, and soon they were feasting on fresh cantaloupe, eggs Benedict, and the most delicious breakfast rolls Sarah had ever tasted. Dan set a tray on the bed between them and poured coffee into both of their cups. The morning paper had come with breakfast, and they each read silently for a time as they applied themselves to their meal. It was a wonderful morning—exactly the kind of morning Sarah wanted to have every day for the rest of her life. Until...

"Damn that woman!" Dan surged off the bed, sending

dishes and cups scattering everywhere. "Of all the disgusting, loathsome, vile creatures . . . She'll wish she'd
never put her fingers on a typewriter before I'm finished
with her!" He was ranting at the top of his lungs, flailing
the newspaper wildly about in one hand as he strode back
and forth across the floor. "How has she managed to live
this long?" he demanded, banging his fist into the back
of a blue velvet wing chair. "How come nobody has
killed her yet? She's got to be stark raving mad if she
thinks I'll stand for this!"

Sarah cowered on the bed, clutching the silver coffee
server, which she'd managed to rescue form the disaster
that was now the bed. Hesitantly, fearfully, she asked,
"Emily Potsdam?"

"Yes!" He swung around to face her. He was standing
in front of the window now, and the morning light came
in behind him, making it hard for Sarah to see his features. All she knew was that his face was very red, and
he was shaking from head to toe. "Yes, dammit! It's
Emily Potsdam! She's done it again. Here"—he shoved
the paper toward her, uttering the foulest oath Sarah had
heard him use—"read this. You might as well see it
now."

Sarah grabbed the paper from him awkwardly, trying
to hold on to the half-full coffee server. She placed the
server on the end table and, with trembling fingers, held
the paper before her, searching the page for the society
column. As she read it her breakfast turned to stone in
her stomach, and only with a great effort did she keep
from throwing up.

Well, friends, he's gone and done it! As much as
we would have liked to have seen him circulating
in Washington society, it seems that Daniel Lowell
will soon be out of circulation—permanently. The
dowry presented by the Ashcroft Nursery was too
good not to be snatched up as part of a package
deal with the beautiful Ms. Sarah Turner as the

main selling point... We certainly can't blame Ms. Turner for securing her own future. There are rumors that Mr. Lowell wanted to buy the Ashcroft property to add to his new town but that Ms. Turner wouldn't sell. As everyone who has ever had dealings with Dan Lowell knows, the man *always* gets what he wants, and at least Ms. Turner has held out for the best possible price. We congratulate her on her good business sense—even if we're green with envy! Couldn't she have left him around awhile longer so the rest of us could have had a chance? All in all, this marriage promises to be the best investment either of the parties has ever made. We wish them the best of luck...

Sarah let the paper fall onto her lap and raised wide, troubled eyes to meet Dan's blazingly angry gaze.

"Can... can she do this?" she whispered.

"Well, she's done it," he said grimly.

Sarah stared back down at the paper, saw the words written in black and white, and knew that tens of thousands of people would be reading them this morning. Suddenly, she knew she was going to be very sick.

Quickly, she got off the bed and, holding her arm around her stomach, made her way toward the bathroom.

"Sarah?" Dan called her name, half angry, half concerned. "Are you all right?"

"I'm... no, I'm not." The bathroom door slammed shut behind her.

Ten minutes later she came out, looking pale and still shaking. Dan was pacing back and forth across the Oriental carpet, waiting for her.

"How are you?" he asked gently, coming up to take her shoulders in his hands. His eyes searched her face carefully.

"Sick," she answered. "Where did she get the idea that you wanted to buy Ashcroft from me?"

Dan looked startled at the question. "Who the hell knows where she got *any* of it?"

"You didn't call her to tell her we were getting married?" Sarah asked.

"Of course not!" he exclaimed. "I was only joking about that."

"Well, how did she find out, then?" Sarah persisted, moving out of his arms to take a few careful steps toward the winged chair. Lowering herself carefully, she closed her eyes and breathed deeply to steady her stomach.

"I have no idea how she found out, but I'm not surprised she did," Dan answered. "One of the prices you pay for being on top is not having any privacy whatsoever. But not even Alicia Mertz could invent such repulsive lies about me. No, Emily wins the prize."

"Do you want the property?" Sarah opened her eyes slowly and looked directly at him. She had to know. The question turned over and over in her brain. She remembered Dan asking her once if she'd ever considered selling it; he hadn't seemed all that interested, but perhaps she'd been mistaken.

Dan stared at her as though she were a stranger. "You believe her, don't you? You think I want your damn property enough to marry you for it!"

"Dan, don't look at me like that," Sarah said weakly. "I had to ask. You don't have to answer me. I don't expect you to. I just had to ask and now it's . . . it's over."

He strode over to the chair where she'd collapsed and squatted down before her, a hand on each arm of the chair. "Is it, Sarah? Is it over?"

There was a long pause. Sarah's eyes were wide as she met his furious gaze. The muscle in his jaw was working hard, and his mouth was a thin line of grim determination. She thought about how quickly it had all happened between them, how she'd been swept off her feet, how devastatingly charming he was—how Emily Potsdam had said he always got what he wanted—and she thought especially about how she'd never been able to resist him . . .

And then she thought about lovely, pure white musk rose blossoms . . .

Tears spilled out of her eyes. "Oh, Dan! I'm so sorry. I don't know what's happened to me. I don't seem to know anymore which way I'm going. I read that horrible article and a disgusting little voice inside my head said, 'What if it's true? What if he only wants the property?' And it made me sick. It made...made me *sick*!" She sobbed and gulped and looked at him through tortured eyes. "Please, Dan. Try to understand what I'm saying. It's all happened so quickly between us, I can't think straight sometimes. I'm sorry for letting you think I doubted you. *Please*..." She choked and held her breath, waiting for some sign that he believed she trusted him. What was the matter with her that she could accuse him of such a despicable act?

Dan watched the agony on Sarah's face, and before too long his own expression softened. "Sarah, I'm going to fix this once and for all," he said. "I'm not going to have us go through this every time somebody takes a shot at me or at us like that Potsdam woman did this morning."

"What are you going to do?" she asked in a tiny voice.

"I'm going to have Leonard Patterson draw up a contract that makes it impossible for you ever to sell Ashcroft to me. We'll put it in trust for our children, or sell shares to the workers, or *something*...I don't know. But I'm going to make it so you're absolutely positive I can't ever take it away from you."

Sarah shook her head violently. "No! I don't want you to do that."

"I'm going to do that!"

"I won't sign it," she warned. "I won't sign something that says I don't trust my own husband not to cheat me. I won't do it! I'd die first!" And she flung herself at him and wrapped her arms around his neck and clung as though she were drowning and he was the only piece of the ship that hadn't yet sunk.

After a minute, Dan relented. "All right, Sarah. We won't talk about it any more right now. Come on and get dressed. We're both late for work."

Sarah nodded mutely.

A half hour later, they rode the elevator down. Dan was grim. Sarah was subdued and still a little pale. When the door whooshed open they crossed the lobby and walked down the wide marble stairs to the front door.

It was a purely instinctive reaction that sent Sarah flying into Dan's arms to bury her face against him as they walked outside and the cameras clicked one after the other in her face.

"What the hell is this?" Dan demanded, holding her tightly.

"Mr. Lowell, is it true that you and Ms. Turner are engaged?"

"Ms. Turner, are you selling Ashcroft Nursery to LINC?"

"What's the date for the wedding?"

"Can we see the ring?"

"Just a minute . . . *Just a minute!"*

It was the hotel manager who saved them. The man was the epitome of cool reserve and calculated determination as he arrived on the scene, turning first to the valet and asking, "Have Mr. Lowell's and Ms. Turner's cars been ordered?" At the attendant's nod, the manager turned again to the reporters and cameramen. "It is not the policy of this hotel to allow its guests to be harassed." He turned to Dan. "I'm sorry you were bothered, Mr. Lowell. Your car will be—"

"Excuse me," Dan interrupted. "I appreciate your concern," he said to the startled manager, "but perhaps it's not altogether inappropriate for me to . . . to make a statement."

Sarah's head jerked up quickly and she looked at him with pleading eyes. "Dan, don't."

He ignored her look and spoke directly to the reporters. "As long as you are all here, I'd like you to witness something. I'll leave it up to the judgment of your reading public as to whether it appears that I'm *transacting business!"*

And without another word, Dan pulled Sarah against

him and kissed her . . . and kissed her . . . and kissed her until she felt her knees go weak and the world swimming around her. She knew what he was doing and felt enraged and at the same time vindicated. It was degrading and cheap to have their lovemaking made so very public. On the other hand, she knew beyond any doubt that nobody watching them could possibly mistake the kiss he gave her as part of a cold-hearted business deal. And she was certain everyone seeing them would have no doubt that Dan Lowell had earned his reputation . . .

She was vaguely aware of the cameras clicking, and there were a few sniggering chuckles in the background; but when Dan finally let her go, there wasn't a sound from any member of the audience. The sidewalk could have been empty for all she knew with her head leaning against him. She couldn't bring herself to look them in the eyes.

Dan heaved a deep sigh and spoke in a low, menacing tone. "Make sure Emily Potsdam gets a copy of that one." Then he looked down at Sarah. "Let's go," he whispered.

Sarah nodded, and they walked straight through the circle of reporters to their waiting cars. Dan helped her into hers, and although he didn't speak to her again, his look said that he wanted her to drive away looking calm and in control. Sarah didn't feel calm and in control; she felt sick. She was mad at him for kissing her for the sake of his own pride, but she was madder at the woman who'd pushed him into feeling that he had to prove himself. And she was maddest at herself for pushing him even further. She'd probably deserved that kiss, and it seemed a small price to pay for doubting him to straighten her spine, hold up her head, and drive past those reporters, looking like she had every right to be outraged over the shadow being cast on her relationship with Dan.

With a slight nod in his direction out the window of her dark red Volvo, Sarah managed a smile that told him she'd be okay.

Dan's rigid expression softened a little and he gave

her a wink before striding over to his Mercedes.

All the way back to Ashcroft, Sarah fantasized about how Emily Potsdam would twist this most recent tidbit of gossip—complete with pictures—into something else to be sick about.

- 8 -

SARAH WENT HOME that evening after work. She had no intention of driving into the District to spend the night with Dan. She wouldn't risk another scene like that morning's. If he wanted to see her, he would have to come to her place. But he didn't come, and when he called late that night, he sounded as though he'd just about dragged himself through the day. They talked briefly about inconsequential things, and Sarah went to sleep feeling no better—and perhaps a little worse—than she had that morning when she'd left him.

The next day Sarah was greeted with the morning paper lying open on her desk, the picture of her and Dan staring up at her from the page. It was Emily's column, of course, and Betty had left it for Sarah to see. Sarah looked thoughtfully at the picture—noted the soft, vulnerable look on her own face and the overwhelming sense of power on Dan's. Even his stance was bold, aggressive, purposeful, while she looked as though she were having a hard time standing up. Well, it had been true at the time. The relationship of their bodies to one another, the complementary expressions of their faces, spoke starkly to her of her deepest fears as well as her deepest pleasures. When they made love—as it would appear to everyone they were doing in the picture—their relationship to one another was exactly right. The picture merely reflected the perfect harmony of their needs for each other. But that same relationship, taken outside of the context of loving, was terrifying to Sarah. When she thought about how vulnerable she'd allowed herself to be to Dan, thought about all the possible ways he could hurt her, her stomach quaked in fear. Even so, she might have overcome her fears, given the mounting evidence that Dan worshiped her, adored her, cherished her—and given time. But there wasn't any time. The world was intruding. Each time she allowed herself to have even a second of doubt about Dan's love for her, she felt her stomach churn and she went cold from head to toe. She felt as though she were being attacked form both sides. On the one hand Dan was showering her with devotion and everything she'd ever wanted to find in love. On the other, there was this shouting throng of people with Emily Potsdam at the head, insisting that it wasn't love at all but something else.

She knew that somehow she had to block out the shouting crowd and forget about Emily Potsdam. With Dan shouting louder and louder that he loved her, she was crumbling under the nearly deafening onslaught from both sides.

A sound from the outer office brought Sarah's attention out of her reverie. Her mouth drew into a thin line as she thought about Betty. Betty had left the paper for her to find. Betty hated Dan. And if the rabble were going to be quieted, Sarah decided, she might as well begin right now to send them home. Grabbing the paper off her desk, she stalked out of her office and came to an abrupt halt in front of Betty's desk.

The older woman looked up. "I see you've had a chance to look at—"

Sarah flung the paper down on Betty's desk. "I've seen it. I don't want to read it. And I don't want you to talk to me about Dan again. Is that clear?"

"Sarah..." Betty began.

"No!" Sarah shouted. "I can't stand it anymore. I've been listening to it from the very start, and I won't listen to it anymore. I don't want to read the morning paper—not this morning, not any other morning. Cancel it. I don't care. Just don't show it to me."

Betty picked up the paper, "Sarah, did you read?"

"No, I said!" Sarah shook her head furiously. *"I don't want to read it!* And I don't want to hear anything more from you about what a fool I'm making of myself or what a cad Dan is or anything else. Now"—she turned and strode toward the door—"I'm going to work. I'll be in the rose fields all day if anybody needs me."

Sarah worked herself into the ground that day. She went home exhausted. When Dan called, he promised he would see her tomorrow, Saturday, and that they'd spend the weekend together. He had an early-morning meeting that couldn't be avoided, but would be out at the nursery by early afternoon.

Sarah agreed dispiritedly, half afraid to face him. She didn't want him to know of her personal struggle, didn't want him to see how badly she had been affected by Emily Potsdam and the reporters and Betty. She fought with herself constantly not to blame Dan for any of it. It wasn't his fault that she was a neurotic mess. He wasn't to blame if she were so weak-willed that she allowed herself to be tossed around by every little bit of idle gossip. She didn't want him to see her feeling so weak; she was ashamed of her lack of faith. He didn't deserve it. He loved her, and his love didn't have anything to do with her nursery stock or her roses or her property...

Did it?

Dan came Saturday afternoon. By silent and mutual agreement, they stayed at Sarah's for the remainder of the weekend. Their lovemaking on Saturday night was different from what it had been, and Sarah didn't like the changes. She had managed to get through the day without being morose and without even thinking very much about the knot of anxiety in her stomach. Yet in the act of love, in which Dan, as always, demanded everything of her—total commitment and complete honesty—she found herself clinging to him desperately, holding on to him as though at any moment he were going to be torn away and that each moment was their last. Sensing the desperation in Sarah's need for him, Dan was at once restrained, reluctant to meet what seemed like irrational fears; on the other hand, he was fiercely possessive, using his body to drive any thought that was not of him out of her mind.

Sarah woke up on Sunday morning feeling exhausted. Dan was withdrawn. The day passed quietly. They spoke of unimportant things and spent most of the day apart: Sarah went down to the nursery for a few hours and Dan chose to stay at the house. She came home to find him slouched in one of the overstuffed chairs in the study, a pen dangling in his right hand, a note pad on the wide chair arm. He was staring moodily into the cold fireplace. When she entered, he rose quickly, saying that he had to be at the office very early and, therefore, planned to drive in that night to avoid the morning rush.

Sarah had to agree that the plan made sense. They had a quiet dinner, and then she watched him go with a mixture of empty longing and relief.

The next day passed with them talking once, briefly, at noon. Sarah got little sleep on Monday night, tossing and dreaming about Dan standing in the middle of her rose garden. She was on the outside of the gate, which he had locked to keep her out.

Thus, when she walked into her office on Tuesday morning and opened the morning paper to the business section—the only section she still felt compelled to read—she was not really shocked by what she found there. It all seemed inevitable. Somehow she'd known all along it would come down to this, and her first reaction was not anger at Dan but complete self-castigation for allowing herself, at thirty-one years of age, to be so stupid.

The headline of the local news section said all that needed to be said: COUNTY COMMISSION RULES ROSE-CROFT MUST HAVE FOURTH ACCESS ROAD. She didn't have to read the rest of the article to know what it would say; it was more an act of self-flagellation that made her look at every word:

> The County Commission passed a ruling late yesterday that makes in necessary for Lowell Industrial Corporation (LINC) to find another access route into its multimillion-dollar new town. Based on the population estimates of both residential and business components of the new town, now being called Rosecroft, the Commission voted by a 4-1 margin to impose the ruling. LINC officials were unavailable for comment, but it is speculated that they have been investigating the possibility of purchasing access rights to the north and northwest of the existing tract. Local contractors scheduled to begin work on Rosecroft are concerned that this ruling will affect the work schedule. Ground breaking is set for July 23, and it is necessary to have the Commission's approval of the overall plan before construction can begin. One local builder is quoted as saying, "I can't believe they [LINC] didn't anticipate this problem. They've had the statistics for months now. Granted, finding the land available for the road is a tough one—property along 208 has been tied up for years. But they should have foreseen the problem . . .

Sarah stared at the print, her eyes out of focus, her face totally devoid of expression. "They should have foreseen the problem . . ." Oh, but they had! They had foreseen the problem—and had employed their deadliest secret weapon to solve it for them.

"Oh, dear God," Sarah whispered in agonized prayer. *"Please* let it be a lie!"

Frantically, she reached for the phone. She had to talk to Dan. She had to hear from him that this was just some horrible mistake. He would make it right. He would explain to her that there wasn't going to be any silly road, that he'd never had any interest in buying her property.

When the phone rang just before she grabbed it, Sarah jumped back as though she'd been bitten. She felt tears spring to her eyes.

"Oh, please be him," she pleaded as her trembling hand reached for the receiver.

"Hello?" she said brokenly, wondering how she'd speak to anyone else . . . wondering how she'd speak to *him*.

"Ah . . . is this the Ashcroft Nursery?" a man's voice asked hesitantly.

Sarah's breath left her in a rush, and her eyes squeezed shut. "Yes," she answered shortly.

"I'd like to speak to Sarah Turner, please," the man said, still hesitant.

"This is she." Sarah sighed, resigned to talking to the man, wanting to get it over with quickly.

"Ms. Turner, this is Leonard Patterson from the legal department at LINC. Dan told you I'd be calling, I believe."

Sarah couldn't make her words form in her brain, much less speak them.

"Ms. Turner?" Leonard Patterson's voice sounded mildly concerned about the odd reception his call was getting.

"Yes, Mr. Patterson, I'm here," Sarah managed to say.

"I want to discuss the written contract terms concerning the sale of your nursery stock to LINC. Dan has told me the arrangements the two of you worked out, and it all seems perfectly fine to me. I plan to use those informal terms to write the contract and simply called to see if you had anything to add." A brief male laugh, and then, "Dan can be very unorthodox in his business practices at times. I thought you would appreciate having things done a little more formally." He stopped, clearly waiting for her agreement or some indication that she was even listening.

Sarah knew she had to get off the phone with this man. This was not the time to be talking about the business deal she'd made with Dan or his unorthodox methods of getting what he wanted.

"I have nothing more to add to the contract," she stated flatly.

"Ah, good, then," Leonard Patterson replied cheerfully. "We were all worried when Dan took off for two weeks before the new offices opened. We were afraid he was deserting the ship!" Again that male laugh. "But my faith in him has been restored. I should have known he wasn't wasting his time."

She *had* to shut the man up and get off the phone! Sarah knew—she just *knew*—that Leonard Patterson would say something that would shatter her world. Any minute now, he was going to prove her worst fears to be true. But something kept her from hanging up. Terrified or not, she had to know the truth.

"Well, Ms. Turner," Patterson was saying, "you and Dan seem to make a good team. I certainly hope the two of you can come to such an amicable agreement when it comes time to talk about the access rights through your property. I'm sure you'll get a good price. Dan's always insisted on that—says you should always give people what they ask for; then they can't complain they got cheated later. He told me this morning that progress was being made in obtaining the rights, so I hope that means we can all reach an agreement soon."

Sarah took the deathblow quietly. A whimper escaped and she closed her eyes against an exquisite stab of pain. She couldn't breathe, and the world swam around her head in a vast whirlpool of sickening blackness. She knew she was going to faint and for a split second didn't care.

It was a single word that saved her. Patterson rambled

on, and something he said caught Sarah's fogged attention. She had no idea what he was talking about, but one word stuck and it galvanized her into getting ahold on herself.

Ashcroft.

This man thought she was going to sign her trees and her roses—and her property—over to Lowell Industrial Corporation! LINC needed *Ashcroft*—to hell with the trees—and Dan had come to buy it. It was all true. Painfully, with lightning speed, the puzzle pieces fell into place. Sarah remembered Dan asking if she'd be interested in selling her land once the nursery stock was gone. When he'd found out she wouldn't sell, he'd gone about getting it another way. And she'd almost let him. Almost.

Very slowly, the knot in Sarah's stomach began to loosen and started to rumble and shake, until her entire being was quivering with unleashed rage. She was fighting for her life, and nothing Dan Lowell did or said was going to keep her from winning.

"Yes," Sarah said quietly, forgetting about the man who was still talking nonsense on the other end of the phone. "He certainly does give people what they ask for."

Leonard Patterson stopped speaking abruptly. "I beg your pardon, Ms. Turner?"

Sarah's eyes narrowed. "I said," she began more loudly, "Mr. Lowell certainly does give people what they ask for. You're absoultely right about that."

"Yes, well...um," Patterson stammered, a bit disconcerted at Sarah's statement. Undeterred, however, he picked up the ball. "Yes, Dan Lowell is an amazing man—a street fighter when he needs to be, but at other times he'll have you signing your life away and think you were getting a bargain. Never met a man like him. No, sir." Patterson took a deep breath and exhaled it in what sounded like a long, envious sigh. "Well, don't you hesitate to call me, Ms. Turner," he urged with patronizing courtesy. "And if you need help in working out the legal aspects of the property deal, that's what I'm here for. I'm sure you must have your own legal counsel, but I hope you know I'll be glad to help in whatever way I can."

"I'm sure you'd be most helpful," Sarah said between tightly clenched teeth.

"Yes... well... we'd like to expedite things and make them as smooth as possible."

"Mr. Patterson"—Sarah's green eyes blazed as she spoke his name—"there's one thing you might just be able to do for me."

"Anything at all," he said in a tone filled with his own sense of importance.

"When you're writing up the landscape contract for me to sign..." she began.

"Yes?"

"...be sure," Sarah continued, "that it says Mr. Lowell can have my trees and the remainder of my nursery stock—and especially the roses—only over my dead body!"

"I... I beg your pardon?"

"Yes, Mr. Patterson, be sure that it's very clear that I will never do business of any kind with Lowell Industrial Corporation. You will have a check in your hand tomorrow morning for the money already paid to me on the contract."

"Ms. Turner! You... you can't do this!" Patterson exclaimed in a panicked voice. "You've made a binding legal agreement."

"I can do it," Sarah retorted. "I *will* do it. And if you don't like it, sue me. Now, if you'll excuse me, I have work to do." She hung up the phone loudly. Then, without pausing, she picked it up once more and dialed her bank. After making arrangements for the draft—thank God she'd spent none of Dan's money—to be picked up that afternoon, she grabbed the keys to her pickup and went to work.

* * *

Dan found her two hours later among the rows of experimental roses. Sarah heard the sound of a car door shutting behind her, and she knew without turning that it was he. She kept on with her work, examining bushes, making notes on the clipboard she carried—praying for all she was worth that she'd be able to get through the next few minutes. Her life depended upon it.

"Sarah!" Dan came up behind her quickly. "I won't let you do this. I'm not going to let you throw it all away because of a ridiculous misunderstanding!"

"Misunderstanding?" she repeated lightly. "I don't know what you're talking about, Mr. Lowell. There's been no misunderstanding."

"You know damned well what I'm talking about!" he barked. "That damned fool Patterson came flying into my office in the middle of a meeting with two contractors, acting like the Russians were coming and he didn't know which way to run first! It took me an hour to get rid of the builders and drag it out of Patterson what happened . . . Sarah, will you for God's sake stop doing that and look at me?"

"I can hear you perfectly well, Mr. Lowell," she said calmly. "I would rather not have to listen to you at all, but short of calling the police to have you removed from the property, I imagine I'll have to. So, let's hear your little speech. I'm immune." She wasn't, but if it killed her, she was going to make him think she was. It would certainly kill her if her performance failed.

"Sarah, stop it!" Dan grabbed her shoulders, and she dropped her clipboard as he spun her around to face him. "You listen to me! I didn't know a bloody thing about that road until this morning! The whole thing came up while I was here with you, taking care of your goddamned roses! I never called in, remember? I didn't care if the whole blasted company went straight to hell while I was gone. The county commission talked to Dale Simon, my vice-president, in my absence and told him they were reconsidering the population studies. Dale had to make moves without me, and it was only when the commission voted that I finally found out!"

Sarah blinked and was silent under his intense gaze. It was easier than she'd expected. She could look at him, and as long as she reminded herself of what an incredible bastard he was, she could suppress the feelings of anguish over the loss of his love—a love she had never really had, anyway. One couldn't miss what one had never had, could one?

"Sarah!" Dan shouted again and shook her, not very gently. "Nobody said anything to me about the problem! There were a million other things going on, and everybody just assumed I knew. And yes, dammit, a lot of them assumed I knew because I've been seeing you. Patterson, Dale Simon—all of them thought I must have been in touch with the commission and found out and come straight out here to meet you. But it isn't true!" Again, he shook her. "You've got to believe me!"

Slowly, Sarah shook her head. "No, Mr. Lowell, I don't have to believe you. I'm going to start doing what I should have done in the first place. I'm going to start believing myself. I'm fully aware that I've been a complete fool. I take full responsibility for my own actions. But let's face it. You are a consummate actor. Never have I seen such a fine performance. I will always base my opinion of any theatrical performance I see in the future upon the one you have given me. It deserves the very highest reviews."

Dan's gaze hardened noticeably. It lost none of its intensity, but began to take on a look of sheer, black rage. "You're saying you think I sold myself to you to get my hands on your property?" he said carefully. "You're calling me a prostitute."

"Oh, no, Mr. Lowell!" Sarah's eyes widened. "I'm calling you a very fine actor. It was very clever of you to convince me of your interest in the nursery stock from the start. It was even more clever of you to insist, in the face of Emily Potsdam's gossip, that you would have both me *and* the stock. A man less confident of his talents would have sworn undying love and refused to buy the stock, rather than risk blowing the whole deal. Making me think you really wanted my trees and roses threw me very nicely off the track. Indeed"—Sarah smiled with saccharin sweetness—"you played the part of a right-eously indignant businessman, as well as the part of a lover, very well. You dedicated yourself wholly to the performance and convinced me in every possible way that you were a man smitten by the arrow of love." Sarah tilted her head to the side and pursed her lips thoughtfully. "Tell me, did you arrange for that little scene at the hotel with the reporters? Did you think I'd like being mauled in public by the rich and handsome Daniel Lowell? Did you think I couldn't wait to be seen with you, to have my name plastered next yours in the paper? And the way you told me you were going to marry me! Why, how very clever you were to make it look like your concern was to protect my reputation! And by the way"—she placed an amazingly steady hand on his chest in a casual gesture—"if I ever get the chance, I promise to tell Emily that her faith in your reputation is by no means unwar-ranted!"

"You're twisting everything I've done and said to fit into some crazy scenario that sounds like it belongs in a late-night thriller!" Dan exploded, his outraged voice booming over the field of bright red roses.

"I believe I have all the facts perfectly straight," Sarah said furiously. "You used me! And you planned it all from the start. I wouldn't even be surprised to find out that you had that devoted secretary of yours compile a dossier on me and the nursery so you could plan the attack well in advance. I'l bet you knew very well my father was dead, although you claimed you didn't. You made a point of saying that Ashcroft being here was a pivotal factor in your decision to buy the tract next to us . . . And maybe it was!" Sarah tossed her head back. "Maybe you thought I'd be an easy target. You wanted another few acres to add to your precious town. Had I ever *considered* selling Ashcroft? you wondered. And you did it oh, so casually."

"Ashcroft was a deciding factor when I bought the tract," Dan barked. "I've made a point for years of know-ing about places that grow roses, but I only knew the names and the reputations," he added defensively, "I came to see your roses! I told you that from the beginning."

"Oh, yes," Sarah drawled as though just remembering. "My roses. Roses just like your dear old mother grew in those humble wooden tubs back in that ugly, nasty city."

Dan's face went ashen, but Sarah continued, ignoring the warning light in his eyes.

"Those poor old bushes with their sweet little buds. Yes, I remember them. Leprechauns and fairies . . . Ha! She grimaced scornfully. "I don't think there ever were any roses—and maybe there isn't even a poor dead mother who fought to deep them alive. I don't think men like you *have* mothers," she hissed. "Only Satan could have raised you!"

Dan's body was racked by one tremendous shudder. His eyes closed tightly, and his voice became a raw whisper. "Sarah, you don't know what you're saying. You've got to stop now and listen to me . . ."

"The only problem was," Sarah interrupted with a sardonic twist of her lips, "your timing was off. A most important thing for an actor, and you should really work on it. You couldn't quite get me to the altar before I found out what you really wanted. Your battle plan didn't take into account the fact that I might not want to sell Ashcroft. Well, you lost time having to reassure me of your complete devotion—time you'd planned to use in order to get me to sign over the deed to my property—not that I think you wouldn't have given me a fair price, mind you!

"This is insane," Dan pleaded, his voice rough with anger and desperation—and something else that Sarah couldn't fathom.

"Is it?" she demanded. "I don't think so. What's insane is that I let myself be totally swept away by a conniving bastard who will stop at nothing—nothing—to get what he wants! *That*'s insane."

Dan's face had taken on a gray cast and he was ominously silent. His hands still gripped her shoulders, and

Sarah felt them tighten. There was a strange look in his eyes that she didn't understand. She was still wondering if he might actually hit her. All of her own energy was being directed toward maintaining her own calculated stand, however, and she wasted no effort in trying to read his thoughts.

A long moment of silence passed between them before Dan spoke, his voice cracked and raw and not at all the mellow, smooth voice Sarah had come to recognize. Somehow this new one went with his new image, and it fortified her to hear him speak—until she heard what he said.

"What about when we made love, Sarah? Was I lying then, too? Was that just a business deal? Would I have been able to make love with any other woman just as convincingly?" He paused, searched her face, shook her a little, and demanded, "Tell me! Would I have touched another woman the same way? Do you think I have such control over my own flesh that no matter whose body was lying beneath me, no matter whose flesh mine claimed . . . that I could have gone through with the act with just as much heart?"

He nearly choked on the last word—and Sarah nearly choked upon hearing it.

For one agonizing moment, she almost gave in. Her hard-won air of indignation wavered in the face of having to admit this final betrayal—the very cruelest of them all. He was right: The whole thing was insane. Nothing had made sense since the day she met him. He'd made her a stranger to herself. Her body had betrayed her, even when all common sense had told her to move carefully. Yes, it was insane. Still, her thoughts and her heart and her body warred inside of her, ripping her apart. An enormous part of her screamed in outrage that she could be killing him right now; that, if she were wrong, the hurt she was inflicting would never heal. Another part of her, the one bent upon self-preservation, said coldly that if she let him convince her again, she deserved what she got, that only the world's biggest fool would fall for the same line yet another time. He knew her too well, knew just where to turn the knife; but her life meant much too much to her to risk it again. She was not going to give in to the desperate, tortured voice that bade her to trust him just one more time—that urged her to seize the chance at love despite all reason and overwhelming evidence that she had not found it yet. Somehow, she was going to survive this. And never again would she be duped by a con artist like Daniel Lowell.

And so, with the greatest effort of will, Sarah shoved aside the soft, feminine longing that she felt had betrayed her and spoke with what she considered cold logic.

"I would say, Mr. Lowell, that your performance in bed had a great deal of heart in it. You know as well as I how utterly convinced I've been. As I said, you are a consummate actor. I can only add that your years of rehearsal for the part have not gone unappreciated."

He would hit her now; she was certain of it. His eyes became strangely bright and hard, and his fingers bruised the flesh of her upper arms as they dug in, His breathing was ragged, and the muscles in his neck and throat worked hard as she watched them in stony silence.

But he didn't hit her. Instead, there was a note of inevitability in his voice as he said, "Then there's nothing left I can say or do to make you believe that I love you."

"I believe," she said quietly, "that you've already said—and done—it all. As difficult as this may be for you to accept, I find your name on a piece of paper stating that you're my husband an unacceptable exchange for my pride and self-respect. The biggest mistake you made, Mr. Lowell, was not realizing that, if you'd been honest with me, I would have *given* you the entire nursery. I . . . I loved you enough to do that. All you had to do was ask." She shook her head and her chin lifted as she added, "But I won't give it to you now. And I won't sell it to you either. If I have to burn every tree on the property, I'll do it sooner than let you have it."

"I could sue you for breach of contract," Dan said coldly. "If I'm such a disgusting bastard, aren't you afraid I'll do it?"

"Go ahead," she snapped. "I'd rather destroy the place

and go to prison for not being able to deliver the goods than give *or* sell you anything ever again."

The sunshine beat down on the roses and on the man and woman standing amidst their riotous splendor. There was no sound. Overhead, a hawk circled. Every second that ticked by was endless.

And over the course of the eternity of seconds, the man's face underwent a change. Slowly, as water draining from a plant that has been uprooted and allowed to dry out in the sun, the anger drained from Dan's face. His jaw relaxed; his eyes lost their hard, unnatural look and came to look merely sad. He sighed. His hands dropped from Sarah's shoulders and hung at his sides. His whole demeanor was one of utter exhaustion and defeat, and Sarah relaxed as she recognized the look, feeling safer now that she knew she'd won. She had won, hadn't she?

"Good-bye, Sarah," Dan said quietly. "I—" He broke off, a spasm of hopelessness and something that looked like frustration contorting his features. And then he simply turned and walked away.

Sarah watched as he got into his car and drove down the long dirt road. When his car had disappeared, she bent and picked up her clipboard and walked to her pickup. She went straight home, took the phone off the hook, and chain-locked the doors. Then she headed up the stairs for her bedroom. She managed to wait until she'd gotten there, but when she saw the bed, she couldn't hold back any longer.

She cried for the loss of an innocence that had only caused her pain; she cried for the mother whom she'd never known; and she cried for Jane Turner who was the only mother she'd ever had. Most of all, though, she cried for the love she'd lost—the love she'd thought she'd finally found. And she hated herself for wishing that she could have gone on believing that that love was real. If only she had let him convince her—just one more time.

- 9 -

HAD SHE BEEN WRONG?

As the summer went by, the question tortured Sarah day after day, night after long, sleepless night. She found herself fighting the same battle an endless number of times—wondering what it could have been like; hating herself for being such a fool about Dan; and hating herself even more because, no matter how much she hated what he'd done to her, she couldn't stop loving him. She'd thrown him out of her life, but she couldn't remove the traces of him from her heart. Still, she refused to give in and admit she could have been wrong. The stakes were too high; she was far too vulnerable. And too many arguments were on her side.

Out of self-defense, Sarah threw herself into work in a way she never had before. It had worked once. It would work again. Ashcroft was the mainstay of her existence—the constant, the glue that held life together. No matter what had happened to her, Ashcroft had been there, and it had needed her. In exchange for care and attention, it had given her shelter, a living, activity to fill the empty hours, and solace in knowing that there was something for which to keep living—in spite of it all.

It was quite simple, really. She went on just as she always had, working ten or eleven hours a day, including weekends. She talked as little as possible to anyone about anything except plants, and carefully avoided private conversation with Betty, whose worried looks proved a daily source of irritation. As she stayed as far away from her rose garden as she could get. It would need weeding and mowing, but she couldn't bring herself to do it just yet. Eventually, she expected time would be on her side and she'd forget. No, she'd never forget; but the sickening, all-consuming pain would go away, and she'd be able to face life again with some degree of enthusiasm.

Several times, she'd taken the letter from Ryan and Roth out of her desk and thought about the job in California. It suddenly seemed very appealing. She loved Ashcroft, but she could hardly stand being there: everywhere she looked, especially in her own home, something reminded her of Dan.

And, too, she was very, very tired of working. She'd known for a long while that the nursery presented her with far more than she wanted to have to do. And now, when her heart just wasn't in it, it was even more tempting to think about taking a job as far away from the place as possible—as far away from Dan as she could get. Yet, each time she'd thought about it, she'd shoved the letter back into her desk and told herself that she wasn't ready to make any major decisions. The hurt was still too fresh. She needed things around her that were familiar and safe until she felt better able to cope with the future. The job would be there; Ryan and Roth had told her that much. She had time. She didn't have to decide yet...

There was one thing she did have to do, however, that could not be put off indefinitely. It was a Saturday morning in mid-July, when the Maryland summer was blazing away at its very muggiest, that Sarah gave in and decided she had to face the chores in her rose garden. After all, the garden had been hers long before Dan had come into her life; it had seen her through both the horrible moments and the victories of her past. It deserved more of her than to be allowed to go untended.

It was quite early when she put on an old pair of cutoffs and a faded blue workshirt, planning to get as much of the weeding and trimming done as she could before the sun had had a chance to climb to its peak. With stoic determination, she picked up her trimming shears and a pair of work gloves from the office and drove the pickup down the long dirt road to the back of the property, stopping before the big white gate.

When she cut the truck engine, there was an unearthly silence. Once, she would have taken her time, enjoyed the solitude, relished the birds' songs and the bright sky and the luscious smells that, even from outside the high brick wall, wafted through the air.

But all Sarah could think about was getting it over with; and so she grabbed her hat and the gloves and tools from the seat alongside her and walked briskly to the gate. She didn't even hesitate when her hand shook on the latch. Nor did she give herself time to think as she pulled the gate shut and walked directly toward the Arrillaga rosebush in the middle of the north wall of the garden.

Out of habit, she began with the Arrillaga when pruning or weeding. Somehow, it was part of the ritual that she tend the garden in the same order in which she and her father had planted the bushes. The Arrillaga was one of her personal favorites, and she knelt down in front of the seven-foot bush, pausing long enough to admire the huge blossoms. She smiled wryly, realizing that her gardener's eye was not entirely jaded; she still thought the pink blooms looked like raspberry sherbet, and good enough to eat. Then, with a tired sigh, she set to work trimming the much-too-high grass back from the bushes in preparation for mowing. It was the backward way of

doing it; that, too, was part of the ritual—weed and trim
first, then mow. Why, she didn't know. It didn't make
good sense; but then, not much did these days.

An hour later, Sarah had made her way to the western
wall and was almost to the gate. Her shirt was drenched,
and she would have taken it off to work in just her bra,
except she would have been blistered by the sun and
scratched with thorns very quickly. She tugged the wet
materials away from her chest and sat back on her heels
to rest a moment. Her hair had slipped down, and she
swept the broad-brimmed hat off her head to fix it, first
running her fingers through the long strands to find all
the pins. She knew she wouldn't last past ten-thirty or
eleven o'clock at the rate the morning was going. She
was cursing the heat and the lack of rain that had made
the ground so hard, and she was starting to feel hungry
when she looked up—hand poised with pin to jab into
the gold knot of hair—and realized she'd worked her
way around to the base of the musk rose that grew just
inside the gate. She let her hair fall and stared.

The huge thirty-foot branches were tied back to the
wall to arch over the gate, although some of them had
been allowed to fall in graceful arches whichever ways
they would. The bush was finished with its annual flowering now, the pristine white petals having long-since
fallen. There were hundreds of them on the ground—
brown, shriveled, but still holding that distinctive smell
that would linger forever in her mind . . . Once more, the
question: Had she been wrong?

Her stomach lurched painfully, and she instantly decided to quit for the day. She considered taking a chain
saw to the entire bush so she'd never have to prune it
again. Sighing, she stuffed her hairpins inside her hat so
she could gather it up for a hasty retreat.

The knock on the gate startled her badly. Sarah stared
at the garden door—her barricade against the world—
for a full half minute before she could answer. And when
she did, her tone was almost surly. Tom knew better
than to bother her there. Still, it must be important . . .

"Come in," she called, and waited as the gate swung open, hesitantly, it seemed.

It wasn't Tom. But Sarah knew immediately who the trespasser was, and the sight of him set her heart pounding.

Michael Lowell looked enough like his brother to be his twin. He was a little shorter and a little tougher-looking, and there was gray in the dark hair. Other than that, only the black slacks and shirt and the stiff white collar of his priestly garb distinguished the man now standing inside Sarah's sanctuary from the one she'd spent an eternity of days trying to forget.

"Sarah? Sarah Turner?"

Thank God, his voice was different. That was her only coherent thought as she continued to kneel, mute and staring, her mouth dry and her hands shaking as they clutched her hat to her stomach.

"Have I got the wrong person?" he asked after half a minute of silence. "Mr. Swenson told me . . ."

"N-no." Sarah shook her head as she finally got to her feet. "I'm Sarah. You're . . . you're Dan's brother, Michael." She knew she was behaving stupidly—rudely—but she didn't know what to think of this unexpected visitor. Had Dan sent him to talk to her? Hardly; one didn't co-opt a priest for wicked purposes, for heaven's sake! But could Michael be here without knowing what had happened between her and Dan?

It seemed that he could. Michael Lowell beamed the familiar Lowell smile as he walked the few yards toward her, holding his hand out and saying warmly, "I've been out of the country at a conference and got home to find Dan's half-a-dozen or so letters telling me all about the two of you. You have no idea what a happy man you've made me, Sarah Turner. I just had to come see for myself that it was really true."

Sarah shoved her gloves and hat into one hand and allowed the other to be taken into Michael's firm grasp. She was sure her palm was sweating and shaking. No, he didn't know the truth. She'd have to tell him.

"Mich—Father Lowell—have you . . ."

"You had it right the first time," Michael said, shaking his head. "If I'm finally going to have a sister, she isn't going to call me Father!"

Sarah smiled weakly. "Have you . . . have you seen Dan since you arrived?"

"No, no. I just got in and couldn't reach him at the hotel. His letters indicated I'd be just as likely to find him here, so I took the chance—wanted to meet you anyway. He looked down at her gardening tools. "I'm sorry if I interrupted your work. If it's inconvenient . . ."

"Of course not," she said quickly. "I was about to quit anyway. It's gotten too hot to do anything here." Self-consciously, Sarah glanced down at her shabby attire and then cast another quick look at Michael. He didn't seem to notice her appearance, though. In fact, he was having a hard time deciding whether to look at her or the garden.

"This place . . ." he began with a slow shake of his head. "I owe Dan an apology. The way he talked about it sounded almost blasphemous, but he may be right. This is really magnificent."

"Thank you," Sarah said automatically. She was about to plunge into some haphazard explanation of the state of things, but Michael once more riveted his attention on her and continued before she had the chance.

"Sarah, you have no idea what a shock those letters of Dan's were to me. Frankly, he's never been serious about a woman in his life—though I'm given to understand he's had his share of, uh, flings. He's certainly never mentioned marriage, and I was beginning to think he never would."

For just a moment, Sarah was thrown off. Her words of explanation caught in her throat, and she said curiously, "Oh?"

Michael chuckled. "He's been married to that company of his for years now. And I must say, he's probably done as much good for others through LINC as I have in all my years in the priesthood. This town of his is just the latest example. Did you know that—" He broke off.

"Well, I probably shouldn't be going on about all that. If you've agreed to marry him, you don't need to be sold, do you, now?" Suffice it to say that as close as we are, you're the first woman he's ever told me about, and it's only fair to tell you that he's told me enough that I think I could write your biography!" He smiled at her warmly, a friendly glint of humor in his blue eyes. Then his smile changed to a curious frown. "Sarah .... something's wrong, isn't there?"

Sarah took a deep breath. She felt her stomach tying itself in knots, felt the tears choking her throat and making it difficult to speak. "Michael, there's something you need to know. There isn't going to...Well, we aren't going to be married." She looked away, unable to face the distressed look on the far too familiar-looking features.

"You aren't..." His voice trailed off. "What happened? Dan was so sure! Don't tell me he's scared you off. I wondered about that—whether he was running true to form, rushing things as he always does. Damn!"

Sarah shook her head a little. "No, that's not exactly the way it is. I don't really think I should be the one to explain. Dan should. It's just that—" She choked, squeezing her eyes shut. Michael's words about Dan had already been enough to shake her resolve. She knew there were now tears streaming down her face, and all she could think about was ending this horrible interview as quickly as possible. "Michael, maybe you'd better go..."

"Sarah." He put his hand on her arm and she flinched. "Come, now. I'd like to hear what happened—from you. Dan sounded so happy, so alive—more so than he ever has. Whatever's gone on must have been devastating. Can't you tell me?"

Sarah forced herself to look at him. "I shouldn't. You're his brother."

"I'm a priest, too, you know. We're good listeners in a crunch."

It was true, Sarah realized. He *was* a priest. And she did so want to talk to somebody...

"Oh, I don't know!" She turned and took several steps toward the center of the garden. "How can I tell you I think your brother is a cad and that he used me and tried to cheat me?"

There was a moment of stunned silence. And then: *"Dan?* You must be joking!" When Sarah swung back, ready to defend herself, Michael waved her off. "No, I see you aren't, and I'm sorry for reacting that way, but . . . well, tell me the rest. There must be some terrible misunderstanding here somewhere."

"I wish that were true," Sarah muttered.

"Come, let's sit over there out of the sun, and you tell me about it." Michael took her arm and Sarah dropped her hat and gloves and allowed herself to be guided toward the bench under the crab apple. He handed her a clean white handerchief, saying, "Now, tell me what Dan has done to you. I know my brother pretty well, and I love him dearly. But I hold no illusions about him either. Just tell me what happened."

And so Sarah did just that. She told him the whole story from the first time Dan had come to Ashcroft. She told him about the landscaping contract and about Emily Potsdam's columns and about Betty's suspicions. She told him about that awful morning with the reporters in front of Dan's hotel, and about how mad Dan had been— or seemed to have been. She told him all her doubts and how confused she had been from the very beginning. And when she got to the worst part,—that nightmarish phone conversation she'd had with Leonard Patterson— she heard Michael's breath catch and then his long, quiet whistle of understanding.

"Saints preserve us, how awful that must have been," he said, just as though he'd been there and knew.

She could only nod. And then she told him about the fight—all of it—every nasty, vicious word of it that she could remember. It seemed to her she had remembered and relived them all a dozen times since.

"And that was the last time you saw Dan?" he asked when she'd finished.

"Yes," she answered. "I wanted him gone. I can't

think when I'm around him. I seem to lose perspective on what's real and what isn't. I couldn't chance his convincing me again that everything was all right." She clenched her fists and banged them on her thighs. "It isn't all right, dammit!"

"Sarah," Michael said, "are you sure it's that you lose yourself when you're with him? Or is it, that you find it impossible to be suspicious or to doubt that he truly loves you then?"

She shrugged, half exasperated. "What's the difference? It all happened so fast, I guess I could never quite believe that it was as good as it seemed."

Michael sighed. "I disagree vehemently that trusting that someone loves you, and losing yourself to some kind of confusion, are the same thing. But I can see where events have led you to feel uncertain about it all." He paused and then sighed again. "For what it's worth, I'm certain that Dan would never have tried to cheat you out of your land. First of all, he's always been somewhat in awe of people who have the landed tradition that you have. He told me the Ashcroft property has been in your family for generations, and I can't tell you how much it means to him that you have that heritage. He doesn't, you know. And he'd never set out to ruin something that he holds almost sacred."

Sarah glanced sideways at Michael but remained silent, feeling that, now that he'd let her have her say, it was fair for him to have his. She only hoped her defenses were strong enough to take it.

"Apart from that fact," Michael continued, his gaze wandering over the garden as he talked thoughtfully, "I'm even more certain that Dan would never marry any woman for any reason other than love. For all the wild stories about him, he was raised in a very traditional and morally strict family. Even if that weren't the case, he's had too many chances for a—a marriage of convenience; there's no reason for him to resort to such methods now."

"There is the access road," Sarah remarked dryly. "That's a reason."

"Pah!" Michael scoffed as though dismissing a trivial

detail. "He's been in worse straits, believe me. Especially when he first started out." Michael turned on the bench then and studied Sarah closely. "The important thing here is that I'm not convinced you really think he would do such a despicable thing. Do you honestly believe in your heart that he doesn't love you?"

Sarah stood up and strode away from Michael's penetrating gaze, wrapping her arms around her middle protectively. "I told you," she said. "I didn't know what to think." If he noted the change in her verb tense, he didn't say anything. "When I got that phone call and read that article, it seemed that my heart had been indulging in a lot of adolescent fantasies and that I was letting myself be made a fool of."

"But now you aren't so sure." So he had noticed. There was a long pause.

"No. I'm not."

"I know it's asking too much of you to go to Dan for an explanation at this point," Michael said gently. "And I'm not sure his response would reassure you anyway. It seems all he's done is make you more frightened." He added, "Which doesn't surprise me, but then he always was . . . Well, let's begin by setting the record straight."

Sarah turned to look at him. Her brimming green eyes held all of her conflicting emotions—a desperation to know the truth, an unwillingness to hear anything that might confuse her further, a kind of stubborn determination to hold onto what was hers, even if it meant unhappiness.

"For starters," Michael went on, "it's true that Dan's known about your nursery for years. He came down here looking forward to meeting your father. I'm sure he was sorry to hear that he'd passed away. Right before I left for my conference, Dan talked about Ashcroft and how pleased he was that he would soon meet Kent Ashcroft, and talk to someone who really knew something about roses, now that Dan had a place to put them. The truth is, roses have always been an obsession with Dan. Mama grew roses and Dan shared her passion for them. I'm

certain that seeing this place must have hit him very hard.
I know it did! He wrote for pages about the garden and
how important it was to you, how you'd planted it with
your father. You'd have thought it was a holy shrine!"
Michael laughed shortly. "Did you know he wanted your
wedding ceremony to take place here? I suppose you
talked about that."

Sarah looked at him sharply. "No. He didn't mention
it."

"Well, perhaps he was afraid to." Michael shrugged.
"He knew how you felt about anyone else being here.
He might have thought it would violate your privacy."

Sarah remained motionless, listening intently but not
offering Michael any encouragement in his effort to explain Dan to her. She studied Michael's friendly, concerned face with great wariness. He was, after all, Dan's
brother. Of course, he would try to defend Dan. But the
fact that he was a priest made her want to trust him.
Certainly he wouldn't deliberately lead her astray! Yet,
she couldn't let him see how strongly his words had, in
fact, affected her. Already, she knew that two of the
things about which she had accused Dan of lying were
true: He had come to Ashcroft to see the roses; and he
had, indeed, had a mother who had meant a great deal
to him.

Suddenly, Sarah wasn't sure she wanted to find out
that she'd been entirely wrong. She'd thought she wanted
to know the truth; but if the truth were presented to her,
would it prove more painful than what she lived with
now?

". . . At the very least," Michael was saying, "you can
bet your life that Dan would never have considered building a road anywhere near this garden. You said the properties join just beyond the south wall?"

Sarah nodded. "The road would have to go through
the garden, unless it took a very circuitous route."

"Well, that's final, then. I think he'd scrap the town
before he'd tear down this garden, even if it didn't belong
to you. As it happens, it does, and"—Michael grinned

engagingly—"he's sure the very leprechauns themselves led him here to find you living in your flowery bower at the end of his rainbow."

She frowned. "He said that?"

"Almost his exact words, and I don't think he would die of embarrassment at your knowing. Mama used to talk about leprechauns and roses and how—"

"He told me," she cut in, hardly able to stand hearing more. She knew she was on the verge of believing Michael Lowell. It was as though Dan were there himself, convincing her as always, smoothing the doubts from her mind with words of love. But Michael had none of Dan's insistent, arrogant manner. It was Michael's utter sincerity that was proving to be her undoing. He couldn't be lying. He just couldn't be. It was unthinkable.

"Sarah," he said gently, "trust yourself. Trust your heart. I don't believe you hate Dan at all. Do you?"

She stared at him, horrified for a moment. "Hate him? My God, I love him so much, it's nearly killing me!" The tears were running again in full force. She made no effort to stop them. "I just don't *trust* him! I'm so confused. I know it isn't possible to love somebody you don't trust—or maybe it is. Or maybe it isn't even Dan whom I mistrust, but the world at large. I just can't believe that anything so good—" She broke off.

"—Could happen to you?" Michael finished cautiously.

Sarah's shoulders sank. "Or could happen at all," she mumbled dejectedly. "And now, if all you say is true— and I don't think even I can really doubt your word . . ." There was a note of bitterness and self-chastisement in her voice—". . . then it's all been for nothing, anyway. I sent him away, and after the things I said . . ."

"Talk to him."

She shook her head, "I can't. He probably never wants to hear my voice again."

"Nonsense," Michael stated flatly. "He must be as miserable as you are. Give him a chance."

"No," Sarah insisted. "I can't expect him to explain.

If I was wrong, then I have to accept responsibility for what I've done. I've accused him, doubted him so many times, it seems... No, he can't want me back."

"Then let me talk to him," Michael suggested.

"No!" Sarah started violently. "No, I don't want him to know we've talked at all! I have to handle this my own way. Please, you have to promise me you won't tell him you've seen me. Please..." She took two steps toward him, desperation showing plainly in her wide eyes.

Michael hesitated. "I don't understand why," he replied slowly, "but if you insist, then you have my promise—as a priest, not as Dan's brother—that I won't say anything about what has passed between us. I'll let you try to work it out. But I want you to promise me that if you need anything, if things aren't going well, you'll let me know."

Sarah smiled with genuine warmth. "Thank you, Michael. I can't imagine why you don't hate me—as Dan's brother, not as a priest," she added at his horrified look, "but I appreciate your coming here and listening."

"You'll let me know what you decide to do?"

Sarah thought for a moment and then answered, "I promise. I realize you can't keep our meeting a secret forever. That's asking too much. Just give me some time to think things through." She paused and then asked, "Are you staying in town for the ground-breaking ceremony next week?"

"I had planned to," he answered.

She nodded. "Give me that much time to decide."

A week later, Michael Lowell found out, along with the rest of the world, just what Sarah had decided to do. She called to tell him to make sure to be at the ground-breaking ceremony. She didn't say why—couldn't because of the bind she was in—but she was sure Dan would need him after it was over, one way or the other.

A few hours later Sarah settled herself on a molded plastic chair in a waiting area of Washington National Airport, a small handbag on the chair next to her, and stared unseeingly at the TV across from her. She was so exhausted, she was afraid she might even fall asleep before her flight was called. It had been the most grueling, gut-wrenching week of her entire life, and she felt more than drained. It was as though she were a sponge and someone had wrung her out and left her to dry until now she was hard and shriveled and utterly useless.

But it was over.

Everything was finished, tied up in a neat package and delivered. Her entire life—that which had been her entire life—was now gone. Nothing remained to remind her of anything in her past. There would be nothing that could haunt the future with memories of the way things were or might have been. Maybe by next week—or next month or year—she'd feel relieved, freed of all her burdens. Right now, all she felt was empty.

Suddenly she blinked and then focused more clearly on the TV screen before her. The six-o'clock news was airing. The bustle of people around her and all the airport noise faded into the background as her attention became riveted on what the newscaster was saying.

"The ground-breaking ceremony for Lowell Industrial Corporation's new town, Rosecroft, held at noon today at the future site of the new LINC offices, contained a few surprises. And it appeared that the person most surprised by the unplanned announcements made by Dale Simon, LINC's vice president, was the president himself, Mr. Daniel Lowell."

The camera cut to a video of the ceremony, and Sarah found herself looking at Dan for the first time in over a month. He was seated on the banner-bedecked platform along with the county and LINC officials in front of a large crowd of spectators. At the podium stood Dale Simon; his face and voice had become all too familiar to Sarah during the past week, and she knew exactly what he was planning to say. Her gaze remained unwillingly, but obsessively, on Dan. She was sure this would be the last time she would see him.

"... The most significant single contribution to the

effort that we are launching today has not come to us through the efforts of any person among us here; nor has it been bought with monies from either the new Rosecroft Corporation or its parent company, Lowell Industrial Corporation. It comes to us as a gift, and we at LINC are duly humbled at both its magnitude and the spirit in which it was given."

Sarah's breath caught at the sight of Dan sitting up a little straighter in his metal folding chair, his attention now glued to Dale Simon's back. She knew he had no idea what Dale was going to announce, and she waited in torment for his reaction.

"As you may have heard, there was at one time considerable talk about LINC purchasing the stock of the Ashcroft Nursery to be used in landscaping Rosecroft. Indeed, the name Rosecroft was chosen on the basis of architectural design that included over fifteen thousand rose bushes. For those of you who don't know, Mr. Kent Ashcroft, the founder of Ashcroft Nursery, spent many years collecting, hybridizing, and selling rare and unusual trees and shrubs, as well as others not so rare but still of the greatest beauty. No one, I am told as a newcomer to the area, ever bought anything ordinary at Ashcroft . . ."

It was obvious that the news station wanted its viewers not only to hear the speech but to see Dan's reaction as well, for they left in all the lengthy pauses during which the audience applauded, forcing Dale to wait. Sarah thought for a minute that Dan looked as if he might stop Dale: He was sitting forward on his seat, and his frown held apprehension and anger in equal measure. Dale hadn't wanted to do it this way, but she'd insisted Dan musn't know until after she'd left town; and LINC's legal department had insisted that the announcement be public. And so she and Dale were both caught in an unpleasant compromise.

"In any event," the unhappy vice-president was saying, "The new Rosecroft Corporation would like to announce the hiring of a very special employee. He is our new grounds manager and nurseryman. For over thirty years, he has worked for the Ashcroft Nursery, first under the ownership of Kent Ashcroft, and since the founder's death, under the ownership of Ms. Sarah Turner, Mr. Ashcroft's daughter and the person who created the landscape plan for Rosecroft. Rosecroft is hiring Mr. Tom Swenson and is pleased to say that his first task—upon completion of the bulk of the construction—will be to carry out Ms. Turner's plan, utilizing the entire stock of the Ashcroft Nursery. Mr. Swenson's service will be paid for, but the trees and the roses are being donated in memory of Mr. Kent Ashcroft, who, his daughter says, wanted them to be enjoyed. And since she has sold the Ashcroft property, she is sure her father would be pleased at the new home his prized plantings will have."

Dan was in shock—that much Sarah was sure of. He glanced around self-consciously, trying without much success to control the emotions passing across his features. Her own heart was beating wildly, for there was more to come. She hadn't really wanted to see this— she had planned to be in the air by now—but she now sat riveted, unable to keep herself from watching.

". . . We are most pleased to join with Ms. Turner in celebrating the work of a dedicated horticulturist and lover of beauty, Mr. Kent Ashcroft. Now, however, LINC wishes to take a moment to thank Ms. Turner herself for yet another gift, which, although made privately, seems to us far too great a gesture to pass over on this day of public celebration. As you know, our ground-breaking is being held only after long and bitter struggle to purchase access rights for a road into Ashcroft."

Sarah saw Dan's lips move and Dale choked momentarily, covering himself by clearing his throat and reaching for a glass of water. He glanced over his shoulder briefly before continuing. Sarah could imagine what had passed between the two men. She didn't envy Dale.

"The rights," Dale continued in a tightly controlled voice, "were finally obtained but are far from satisfactory for our purposes. However, we have been given another choice—a far superior choice. For along with the stock of her nursery, Ms. Turner has deeded, free and clear to the Lowell Industrial Corporation, a strip of land that runs from the northern boundary of her property on Route 208, where the nursery offices and greenhouses themselves are now located, south to the northwest boundary of Rosecroft..."

Suddenly, Dan hunkered back, legs crossed, his forehead resting on one hand in a posture that suggested extreme distress.

"...This land, has been given to us pending the satisfaction of a single condition of the contract." Dale straightened and tugged nervously at his collar. Clearing his throat, he continued, "That condition states that the walled garden that sits on the property in question—and is, in fact, located between the Rosecroft boundary and the main road—shall be preserved intact. The road shall be built to the east of the garden, passing it at a distance of no less than three hundred yards. There now exists a separate property deed for the garden, and this, Ms. Turner has expressly stated, is to be given to Mr. Daniel Lowell for his personal use and enjoyment of the property described therein. LINC has made this announcement in spite of Ms. Turner's desires to keep the donation a private one because it was felt by our legal department that, since the garden would ultimately be in a vulnerable position, we couldn't fulfill the terms to protect it unless..."

Dale's words faded out in a blur of tears and pain. Sarah watched in agony as Dan uncoiled from his protective cage and surged to his feet. The look on his face was like a knife stabbing through her heart. It was what she deserved, she knew. But in the futile hope that he would understand the gesture, she had made it—all the while loathing the public manner in which it had to be done. It seemed to her now that the gift had been—like all else—for nothing. If there was understanding on Dan's face, she couldn't see it. All that was obvious was his complete rage.

The video ended with him striding off the platform, his fists tightly clenched, the officials seated on the platform staring after him in confusion.

"There was much speculation after the ceremony—and it will probably go on for quite some time—as to the full meaning of Ms. Turner's generosity." The newscaster wore a somewhat smug and knowing smile as he continued his piece. "Mr. Lowell was not evasive in his comment, however, and said to reporters that he . . ."

"TWA flight 347 now boarding at gate seven . . ."

Three people walked between Sarah and the screen, hauling a copious amount of luggage, including a small dog, which was yapping unhappily inside its carrier.

It was enough to break the spell. Quickly, Sarah grabbed her handbag and shakily got to her feet. The long walk to the boarding ramp passed in a kind of hazy, surrealistic dream. Faces, walls, and doorways swam before her like something out of a Fellini film—the very stuff that nightmares are made of.

And, indeed, Sarah's nights were filled with that stuff for some time to come.

- *10* -

THE SEA OF boxes was endless. It seemed as though they would never be emptied, and if they were, that there would never be enough cupboards, closets, and shelves to hold their contents. Sarah wiped the back of her hand across her forehead and then rubbed her palms on the legs of her old jeans. She didn't know why she had thought it wouldn't be as hot in northern California as it was in Maryland. And she scolded herself for the dozenth time for not bringing the air conditioner Dan had bought. She hadn't wanted to have anything to remind her of him in her new life, but as she put a hand to her aching head and felt the heat there, she wondered if she couldn't have lived with just that one reminder.

Moving much more slowly than she had that morning when she'd begun to unpack, she picked up another box that contained her grandmother's dishes and started gingerly up the stepladder that she had placed under the hole in the hallway ceiling. The hole led to the attic crawl space, where she hoped to store most of the boxes she didn't need to unpack.

When the moving van had left her house in Maryland, Sarah hadn't really been able to take in the magnitude of the chore that would await her at the other end. And she was glad she'd gone to Oregon first, leaving the movers to their own and the landlord's devices while she visited with the Turners for a week. She felt better able now to face the unpacking process, which she still had another ten days to accomplish. It was Friday, and Ryan and Roth weren't expecting her to start work until a week from Monday . . .

Sarah moved the box she carried up the ladder one rung at a time. Finally, standing on the step just below the top, she was able to shove the box up into the attic. Why on earth she'd rented an apartment on the third floor of a hot old place like this when she could have had an air-conditioned, modern apartment, she'd never know. No, that was a lie; she'd rented it because the house reminded her of home. It was Victorian and had high ceilings and a porch around three sides. Well, now she was paying the price of sentimentality.

The knock on the door provided the one hopeful note of the day. She'd been expecting the telephone company to come hook up the phone.

"The door's open!" she called, leaning down to shout out the hole in the ceiling. "Come on in. I'll be down in a minute." She leaned against one side of the crawl space and studied the situation in the dimly lit attic. There was still enough room for a dozen or so boxes if she stacked them carefully.

Holding on to the attic floor, she felt with her foot for the next rung down the ladder. "I hope you can find the wall," she said with a laugh, bending down to look for the phone company worker. "I'm sorry the boxes are—"

Sarah choked back a gasp, nearly lost her footing on the next step, and caught herself by wrapping both arms around the ladder and clinging for dear life.

"Dan!" she whispered. "What—?

"I see you're still inviting mad rapists in through your door," he remarked casually, and then, eyeing her precarious position: "Didn't anybody ever tell you you aren't supposed to stand on the top step of those things?" He leaned against the door frame between the living room and hall just three feet from her and let his gaze roam over her in cool appraisal.

"Why . . .?" Sarah couldn't decide which of the questions pounding in her brain she most wanted to ask. Why was he there? Was he going to throw the deed back in her face the way she'd thrown his love back in his?

"Get down off the ladder, Sarah," he said calmly. "What we've got to talk about is best said with both feet on the ground."

Her eyes widened and after a moment's hesitation she stepped down obediently, if unsteadily. He let her stand wondering for a long time. They simply stared at each other. And in spite of her quaking insides, Sarah drank in the sight of him. He looked tired, yes, but calm and relaxed, and the sparkle in his blue eyes was very bright. He was dressed casually—dark slacks and a white terry pullover unbuttoned at the neck. Sarah's eyes feasted longingly on the broad shoulders and the hard planes of his dearly remembered body. When she couldn't stand the silence and the looking anymore, she whispered, "Dan . . . please." She looked away, unable to meet his unrelenting gaze any longer. "Why did you come?"

"Why do you *think* I came?" he asked in response.

She shook her head violently. "I don't know!" And then, quickly, she added, "You can't give me back the trees. They were to be a memorial to my father and there must be a law somewhere that says you can't return things like that. If it's the land you've come about, it belongs to your company and you'll have to argue with them if you don't want it. I don't care what you do with it— sell it to Joe Miles, if you want. I just thought . . ." She closed her eyes and swallowed hard against the rising tears. "I thought you might want the garden. If you don't,

then . . . then . . . " She ended in a hoarse whisper, unable
to tell him to tear it down, unable to say she'd take it
back.

"Sarah . . ." Dan's voice still had that calm quality
about it. It held patience and tenderness in equal measures.

Sarah opened her eyes and looked at him. Then she
had to bite her lower lip to keep it from quivering. Quickly,
she wrapped her arms around her middle and brushed
past him into the living room to walk the straight path
through the boxes and stand in front of the curtainless
bay window.

"Why did you come?" she asked again. "I suppose I
can't begrudge you the right to give me back some of
what I gave you. Please. Say whatever you have to say
and leave."

"Sarah," Dan said yet again, and then, slowly, one
step at a time, walked across the room to stand behind
her. "I came to tell you that you cheated me."

Sarah whirled to face him, stunned. "Cheated?" she
said, trembling.

He nodded gravely. "I've got your trees, and I've got
your land, and I've got your roses. But it seems to me
that the price you're asking me to pay for it all is far,
far more than I can afford."

"Wh . . . What price?" she asked, mesmerized by his
gaze.

Dan gave her a thoughtful look. "I figure the only
way to make things fair is for me to give you back what's
yours and you give me back what's mine."

"But—" Sarah began. "But I haven't got anything . . ."

"Oh, yes you do," he insisted, "and it's got nothing
to do with those beds of roses."

Sarah felt tears stinging her eyes and her throat closed.
She'd give him anything—anything at all—if it would
make up for what she'd done to him. "What do you
want?" she asked weakly.

"What do you *think* I want, you idiot?" he asked with

a lazy, crooked grin. "If you've got to hear me say it: I want you!"

A tiny sob escaped her and the tears spilled down her cheeks. She couldn't have heard him correctly. He couldn't possibly mean it—even though his eyes, his mouth, everything about the way he was looking at her, said it was true.

"How can you still want me?" she cried, shaking her head in refusal. Soon, soon now, he'd tell her it was all a joke to make her pay...

"Sarah," Dan crooned, taking a step toward her, "I never stopped wanting you."

"That day in the rose field," she began again, "that day I said all those horrible things to you...How can you ever forget what I said? How can you still want me after that?"

"I stopped being angry about what you said before I ever left the garden," Dan replied sadly. "It was very, very clear that it hurt you as much—more—to say it than it did for me to hear it. You were angry and you hated me, but you were dying inside because you thought I didn't love you. And the worst pain I've ever had in my life was in knowing there wasn't any way I could make you stop hurting. I couldn't make you believe me; you had to do that yourself."

Sarah's eyes closed and quickly she covered her face with her hands, wanting to hide an abiding sense of guilt. She hadn't changed her mind—Michael had. Deep inside, she knew that had it not been for Michael, she would always have tortured herself over whether she'd accused Dan falsely. As Michael had pointed out, her heart had known, even when her head had been mixed in confusion. But she'd always live with the knowledge that she'd let that confusion blind her, cut her off from her own intuitive sense of the truth.

Sarah wondered if she'd spoken her shameful thoughts out loud when Dan said, "Sarah...My darling Sarah, it doesn't matter how you came to see the truth." His hands closed gently around her wrists. "Sarah, do you hear me?" He waited a moment and then pulled her hands away from her face and tilted her chin up until she met his gaze. "It . . . doesn't . . . matter how you found out." He emphasized each syllable and filled each with meaning. "Do you understand what I'm saying?"

Sarah looked at him hard and held her breath. He knew. Well, of course, he knew. Michael had been at the ceremony and they had talked . . .

"Michael told you," she said.

"He didn't have to," Dan replied. "He was at the ceremony just as you had told him to be—which is a damned good thing. All he had to say was that he'd met you; I knew what had happened."

"I saw the ceremony on the news," she whispered brokenly. "You looked terribly angry."

"At Dale, yes. I was furious until I found out why he had to do it the way he did and the bind the legal department had put you both in. But I was never angry at you, Sarah."

She looked at him wonderingly, disbelievingly.

"I knew the instant the words were out of Dale's mouth what you were saying," he continued, his eyes caressing her tenderly. "And if I hadn't been so hell-bent mad, I would have cried. I left because I didn't think I could stay angry enough not to dissolve into tears, right in front of all those people."

She stared at him a moment longer and then shook her head violently, unwilling to forgive herself even if he had done so. "If Michael hadn't come that day . . . Dan, I don't know if I would ever have . . . "

"Darlin', it doesn't matter what made you change your mind."

"How can you say that?" she cried. *"How can you forgive—?"*

"Sarah! *It doesn't matter!*" he shouted her into silence. "If I'd thought of it, I would have had Michael come myself—long before! But I didn't, and I can only thank God—and maybe some other forces—that Michael came on his own."

She had to blink back the tears several times. "It doesn't matter? You don't care that—?"

"No!" Dan barked. "I don't—" He stopped short. "No, that's not right. I do care. I'm *glad* Michael came and told you what a complete fool I am over you. And I don't want to have to say it another time! And why in the hell are we standing here arguing when I haven't held you in so long I could die?"

"Oh, Dan," Sarah managed rather breathily before he had her in his arms and his mouth found hers. They clung to one another, sobbing and gasping and speaking each other's name in chanted whispers.

"Dan," Sarah sobbed, "I won't ever be able to make it up to you! I knew inside—I knew you loved me but I was sooo scared! So many things had happened—Emily Potsdam, Betty, Joe Miles calling to tell me he'd like the first crack at buying Ashcroft . . . So many things making me feel like the whole world was turning upside down and I was spinning in circles, wondering which way to go!"

"I know, mavourneen, I know," he soothed, his voice as filled with emotion as her own.

"I read about the road in the paper, and it frightened me to death. I was going to call you. I swear I was! But Leonard Patterson called before I could pick up the phone. He was so sure, Dan—so sure I knew all about the road and that you and I had talked about it. He said . . . he said you'd told him you were making progress on the deal. He assumed I'd agreed to it and it made it sound—"

"I know how it sounded," Dan broke in. "I know that Leonard Patterson is never going to have the chance to make assumptions about me again. I fired him that morning. Too damned many people have made wrong assumptions about me. I've listened to it and read about it for years, and I can't promise it won't continue, Sarah." He held her away from him and, cupping her tear-streaked face in his hands, locked her gaze with his. "People like Emily Potsdam and Leonard Patterson—there are people everywhere who jump at the chance to make a man in my position look bad. Or maybe, like Patterson, they're just trying to elevate their own egos by having others think they know what's going on, that they're in some way connected to the inner circle . . ." He tossed his head back in frustration, then looked at her with soul-piercing intensity. "Sarah, I can do a lot of things, but I can't make people stop saying things about me, good or bad."

"Oh, Dan, I know!" Sarah cried. "And I hate myself for listening! I hate myself for joining in, for not being strong enough, for making you think I didn't love you." She took a great gulp of air and said emphatically, "I never stopped loving you, though. Not ever!"

"Oh, Sarah—"

"I just didn't know what to think," she continued. "I was so afraid that I was getting sucked further and further into a trap and that I'd never escape. Dan, nothing's ever happened to me so fast and so *strongly* before. I never, ever expected to have somebody love me the way you did!"

"Do," he corrected. "Sarah, I don't blame you for being confused. I don't blame you for anything."

"How can you—?"

"Hush." He stopped her with the light brush of his lips against hers. "Listen. I found out something the last few weeks. I found out, after years of raving like a maniac every time somebody like Alicia Mertz or our own Emily would take a shot at me, that I didn't care what they said. When I met you, I stopped caring about what anyone thought. The only opinion that mattered was yours. As long as you believed in me, the world was sane."

Sarah whimpered, knowing she deserved this torture and somehow welcoming it.

"When it turned out that all those other people still mattered to *you,* I was furious." Dan sighed wearily at the admission. "I don't know that I even realized it consciously, but I knew it made me want to kill to think you might become infected with others' thinking about me. When I actually saw signs of it happening, I was frantic. I did everything I could to drive it out of you. That morning I kissed you in front of the hotel, I'm not sure whether I was more upset about the damned newspaper article or about the fact that you actually seemed to take it seriously. It was wretched to subject you and our love to public inspection."

"Dan, don't—"

"I behaved like a madman most of the time we were together."

"Dan, no!"

"It's true! It's no wonder you felt confused. The louder Emily and company hollered, the harder I tried to batter you from the other side. Everybody, including me, has been playing football with your heart, and it's a miracle you didn't run away from us all." He broke off, looking around at the strange, empty apartment and the stacked boxes. "Good lord, what am I saying?! You *have* run away, haven't you? Sarah, I never meant to ... Oh God! I'm sorry!"

Sarah's hand left his shoulder to touch his face. She saw the pain and the remorse etched on the handsome features she so loved, and she could hardly believe she was being given absolution for her sins. He wasn't blaming her; he wasn't going to hold it against her that she'd been a weak-willed traitor. She might still blame herself, but the relief of hearing him admit his part in the thing was equalled only by the love she felt pouring out of her heart, a love that communicated itself to him in the vulnerable, liquid look in her eyes and the touch of her hand upon his face.

"I didn't run away," she said softly. "I couldn't allow myself to sit there at Ashcroft and hope that you might still love me, that you might someday forgive me. I had to get on with my life."

"Sarah ..."

"I'd been thinking of taking this job with Ryan and Roth even before I met you. It seemed like a good thing to do—under the circumstances."

"Sarah," Dan said, "I've made a fortune out of nothing, and I know I'm good at knowing what to say and when to say it—at knowing how another person thinks and how to use what I know. I think when I met you I must have pulled out all the stops, I wanted you so badly!"

"Dan . . ."

"Mavourneen, I don't ever want you to feel that I've targeted you for a killing as I would a competitor." Dan's face was tortured as he finished roughly, "I can survive a lot of things, Sarah. But I've learned that I don't want to survive without you. Nothing I've got makes any difference unless you're there to share it with me. Oh, God, Sarah!" His eyes closed as he said softly, "Please come home with me. Please let me love you."

"Oh, Dan, yes!" Sarah threw her arms around him, and once more they were overcome by the need to speak with their bodies what their eyes, their words, their hearts, had been saying.

Neither could quite get over the realization that they were being given a second chance, that love had not deserted them but had found a way to survive in the face of all odds.

Dan's mouth and hands couldn't get enough of the feel of Sarah's body. Sarah melted under his touch, clung to him blindly, lost in the unending power he had to make her feel things she'd never known existed before he'd shown them to her. His mouth tasted so good on hers! His hands on her face, her back, her breasts and hips, were rough and tender and shaking with need. And the love and passion she'd tried so hard to forget were welling up inside of her in joyous response. All at once, all that denied feeling—all those crushed dreams—swept up to catch them both in a vortex of such magnitude that Sarah gasped and Dan trembled at the impact. It was immediate, urgent in its demand to be satisfied.

Without even realizing what was happening, Sarah found herself being lifted from the floor and carried. The stepladder clattered against the wall when Dan shoved past it. Then Sarah's feet were lowered once more to the floor. Her clothing was being nearly torn off of her, and her fingers didn't hesitate to do the same to Dan's. She

had to touch his bare flesh beneath the layers of cloth,
and she sighed in sheer ecstasy when at last she found
that longed-for male body. His mouth was everywhere
upon her, tasting of her own mouth, kissing a trail down
her neck, covering her breasts one after the other until
she leaned against him, unable to bear the nearly painful
pleasure any longer, her hands holding his dark head
cradled to her, praying he would never stop.

The bed felt solid and very much like home when she
found herself upon it. And when she held her arms out
to receive the cherished burden of her lover's body, she
sank deeper into its welcoming depths.

There was no waiting or prolonging the union—no
need to pretend they wanted anything but to fuse their
flesh and their souls into one—immediately, yesterday,
forever. It was joyful, painfully sweet, and almost violent. Sweat mingled with tears. Gasps turned to deep,
soul-shattering groans. And the endless wave that seized
and carried them both emanated from but one source.

"You're coming back with me," Dan said much later.

"Hmm," she murmured her assent.

"Michael's still there. He'll stay for the wedding. If
it's okay with you, I'd like him to marry us. In the
garden..."

"Absolutely," Sarah replied. And after a moment's
contented silence, she added thoughtfully, "I'd like to
find a place to live besides your hotel. I mean, not that
it isn't..."

"What's the matter with the house you've got?" Dan
broke in.

"I sold it," she answered gloomily. "I would have
thought Betty had told you—along with everything else.
She *is* the one you conned into telling you where I was,
isn't she?"

"Don't you dare speak a word against that sainted
lady," Dan chided.

Sarah looked up at him in bewilderment. "Sainted
lady?"

"Uh-huh." He nodded. "It seems she doesn't hate me

after all. She just thought you ought to exercise a bit more, uh, caution. She was so upset about how you've been, and even more upset about your selling Ashcroft, that once I'd persuaded her of my honorable intentions"—he grinned—"well, it was an easy matter to get her to tell me where you'd gone."

"Hmph!" Sarah pouted, eternally grateful that Betty had betrayed her.

"By the way," Dan continued, "for your information, you did not sell your house."

"I beg your pardon, but—"

"You sold the land it sits on," he explained patiently. "And, bless his greedy soul, Joe Miles doesn't give a damn about old Victorian homes. All he's interested in are town houses and split-levels. He wouldn't sell me back the land, but he *gave* me the house."

Sarah frowned. "With access rights?"

"Nope. Wouldn't give over a parcel along Route 208."

For the life of her, Sarah couldn't think how a land-locked house would do them any good. "So?" she said when she got tired of trying to solve his riddle. "What good does—"

"A house," Dan began airily, "in any other place would look as . . . neat?"

"Ohhh," Sarah groaned. And then the impact of his terrible misquote hit her. She rose up on one elbow and looked down at his relaxed and happy face. "You *moved* it?"

He nodded affirmatively. "Cost a fortune."

"But where did you put it?"

"Dead center of the strip you deeded to LINC. It looks a little strange right now between the rows of bigleaf magnolia and Russian olives, but they'll be gone soon, and then we can landscape the lawn with good old-fashioned white pine."

"My father would roll over," Sarah grimaced. She was about to lie back down, but another thought occurred to her. "So what good does moving the house there do? I don't own the land anymore. There's going to be a road on it . . . isn't there?"

"Yes you do, and no, there isn't, unless it's our own driveway. I bought the land from LINC and deeded it back to you."

Sarah's eyes widened in astonishment and awe. "How did you talk them into that? I thought they needed the land badly."

"They do, " he agreed. "But, Sarah, me darlin'"— Dan gave her a hurt look—"have ye no more faith in me pow'rs of persuasion than that?"

"Don't ever—ever—ask me that question again." Sarah shivered.

"Well, then, it should be easy for you to understand." He shrugged one bare shoulder. "It was quite simple, really. In the first place, you deeded the propety to Lowell Industrial Corporation. And, Sarah, I *am* Lowell Industrial Corporation." He graced her with one of those arrogant smiles of complete assurance and total male charisma. "In the second place, when the board and the planning committee appeared reluctant to let me have the strip, I merely pointed out that it was worthless." He paused and waited expectantly for her next question.

"All right, all right," said Sarah indulgently. "And how did you make it worthless? The last time I saw it, it looked okay to me." She could see he was enjoying his little melodrama immensely, even if she was on pins and needles, waiting to hear the conclusion.

"Well," he drawled, "let's say I rendered the land useless to them as far as an access road went."

"And why is the property useless . . . ?"

"Because Rosecroft and Ashcroft no longer adjoin."

She stared at him, totally confused. "Now you're going to tell me that, in the last four days, you've had a lake dug right across the boundary line."

"Better than that." He smiled secretively.

Sarah's eyes took on a fearful look. "Oh, Lord, Dan! What did you do?!"

"You told me once or twice that the only thing you'd be happy seeing on the other side of the garden was—"

"You didn't build a cemetery?"

"I didn't," he explained carefully, "but the church that owns the property is going to. I made it the only condition of the gift."

Sarah's jaw dropped open. "Tell me you're joking."

"Oh, no. I'm very serious, " he assured her. "I bought five acres of land from LINC at a price that would give them funds to buy another small strip to add to the one they'd had to settle for at the last minute. Then I gave it all to a happy little congregation of Episcopalians. They're going to put a new church on the southeastern corner—far, far away from the garden. And the rest of the acreage, they're going to use for . . . well, for resting," he finished with a self-satisfied sigh.

"Oh, dear." Sarah grimaced at his pun, but she had to laugh at his self-congratulatory expression. "I'm afraid to ask what else you've been up to. You've had a busy time since the ground-breaking ceremony."

"Torturous would be a better way to describe it," he corrected cheerfully. "First, I had to disappoint Dale Simon and take the Rosecroft project away from him. Then I had to convince the hotel to give me back my suite and unpack my suitcases. All that was easy."

"What are you talking about?" Sarah asked, feeling her head reel in a wonderfully familiar way as she listened to him.

"I had decided to go back to New York. I wouldn't have stayed in D.C. another day after ground-breaking. But you changed all that, so . . . back to work I went. In between three-hour sessions with the county commission and the water and sewage company and everybody else and their brother, I made phone calls to Joe Miles and house-moving companies and had meetings with land-hungry ministers. The hardest part was convincing Joe Miles to part with some of the land you sold him. I paid him twice what he paid you for it, and he wasn't altogether happy about that."

"You *did* buy it back!" Sarah exclaimed with an inward groan, wondering what the total cost would be for undoing all of what she'd so painstakingly done before she'd left Maryland.

Dan read her thoughts immediately. "Don't ask me what all this has cost. Just be glad I can afford you. Unfortunately, however, no amount of money would part Joe Miles with the Ashcroft property. I got some, but not all." He shrugged. "After talking to Tom Swenson, I wasn't worried, though. He said you wouldn't need more than the tract you deeded to LINC—the one I got back—plus the piece I got from Miles, which adjoins it."

"This is starting to sound like 'The House That Jack Built,'" Sarah muttered. "And what is it I'm not going to need more land for?"

"Do I have to tell you everything?" He gave her a reproachful look. "Growing roses! That *is* what you do, isn't it?"

Sarah's grin was impish. "You mean the wife of Daniel Lowell, land baron and every woman's dream, will have time to do something besides keep up with his crazy schemes. Or"—her eyes narrowed to twinkling green lights—"is it that you're worried I might get bored waiting up for you to come home every night at eleven?"

Dan raised a brow. "If you think I'm going to be working until eleven at night when you're home waiting for me, you're out of your mind. And, well, of course, you can do whatever you damned well please . . . grow roses or not grow roses—except . . ." He looked at her questioningly, and his words became strangely hesitant. "Except it would be nice if you could find the time to have a baby or two. I mean, I'm thirty-nine years old, and I'd like to think . . ." He trailed off with uncharacteristic uncertainty.

Sarah smiled tenderly. "One of the first things I did after I sent you away was to throw away my pills. I haven't been taking them for weeks now."

It was Dan's turn to look stunned. "Sarah?" His eyes searched her face and then roamed down over her glowing, naked body lying so close to his.

"I could be, but I'm probably not," she whispered. "Still, I'm not going to take the pills again, unless you want to wait."

He shook his head slowly.

"Good." She grinned. "So I get to live in my very own house on my very own land and grow my very own roses and *our* very own children! What more could I possibly ask for?!"

"Well," Dan chuckled, "I have one request. If you can spare the space between the hybrid teas and the floribundas, I'd like to have a swimming pool. If I'm going to survive the Maryland summers, I need all the help I can get."

Sarah plopped back down on the bed to lie on her back. "Of course," she replied automatically. And then she frowned up at the ceiling. "One more thing. I'm confused."

"So, what's new?"

"Don't you start," she warned. "You're enough to confuse anybody. What I want to know is, if I gave the land to LINC, and the deed said I gave it on the condition that there be a separate deed for the garden and that that be given to you, but you bought the land back from LINC and deeded it to me . . . who owns the garden?"

"Technically, you do," he answered. And he turned on his side to face her, throwing an arm across her stomach as he did so. "But if you want to give it back to me as a wedding present, I won't refuse. In my heart, it will always be mine, now. You're giving it to me was an utterly perfect act of love, and it saved my life." His lips brushed hers tenderly.

"It's yours," she said gently. "I'll grow roses for you forever if it'll make you happy."

Dan's eyes met hers in a promise-filled caress. "Mavourneen, I've been waiting a long time for the roses to bloom and my dreams to come true. I came to you that first day asking for roses—but needing love. And there you were." His finger traced her parted lips, touched them with his own. "You *are* my love and my roses, Sarah. As long as I have you, I won't need any others."

And they sealed their final contract in a most unbusinesslike fashion, both more than satisfied with the terms of the agreement.

Second Chance at Love ®

QUESTIONNAIRE

1. How do you rate _____
   (please print TITLE)

   ☐ excellent   ☐ good
   ☐ very good   ☐ fair   ☐ poor

2. How likely are you to purchase another book
   in this series?

   ☐ definitely would purchase
   ☐ probably would purchase
   ☐ probably would not purchase
   ☐ definitely would not purchase

3. How likely are you to purchase another book by
   this author?

   ☐ definitely would purchase
   ☐ probably would purchase
   ☐ probably would not purchase
   ☐ definitely would not purchase

4. How does this book compare to books in other
   contemporary romance lines?

   ☐ much better
   ☐ better
   ☐ about the same
   ☐ not as good
   ☐ definitely not as good

5. Why did you buy this book? (Check as many as apply)

   ☐ I have read other
     SECOND CHANCE AT LOVE romances
   ☐ friend's recommendation
   ☐ bookseller's recommendation
   ☐ art on the front cover
   ☐ description of the plot on the back cover
   ☐ book review I read
   ☐ other _____
     _____
     _____

(Continued...)

6. Please list your three favorite contemporary romance lines.

_____
_____

7. Please list your favorite authors of contemporary romance lines.

_____
_____
_____
_____
_____
_____

8. How many SECOND CHANCE AT LOVE romances have you read? _____

9. How many series romances like SECOND CHANCE AT LOVE do you <u>read</u> each month? _____

10. How many series romances like SECOND CHANCE AT LOVE do you <u>buy</u> each month? _____

11. Mind telling your age?
        ☐ under 18
        ☐ 18 to 30
        ☐ 31 to 45
        ☐ over 45

☐ Please check if you'd like to receive our <u>free</u> SECOND CHANCE AT LOVE Newsletter.

We hope you'll share your other ideas about romances with us on an additional sheet and attach it securely to this questionnaire.

• •

Fill in your name and address below:
Name _____
Street Address _____
City _____ State _____ Zip _____

Please return this questionnaire to:
   SECOND CHANCE AT LOVE
   The Berkley Publishing Group
   200 Madison Avenue, New York, New York 10016